A Thousand Love Letters

Shwetabh Gangwar

Vitasta
Let Knowledge Spread

Published by
Renu Kaul Verma
Vitasta Publishing Pvt Ltd
2/15, Ansari Road, Daryaganj,
New Delhi - 110 002
info@vitastapublishing.com

ISBN: 978-93-82711-15-5

Typeset & Cover Design by Vitasta Publishing Pvt Ltd
Printed by Vikas Computer and Printers

Chapter - 1

15 December, 2004

Dear Love,

If there is anything that can explain my love for you in a better way than this letter today, then I am not a true lover. I never realized that this part of my life could be so daunting, so saddening; as I always believed love is kind, patient, and motivating. I didn't know the cause of these tears as they looked unreal to me, until today, when even the air I breathe has a memory of you. I can no longer say that I knew what true love was, for I had never understood it until I met you. Now that I am a victim of it, and trapped by it, I have felt what a heart is, and what a true lover feels. Now, I feel real pain and fear, for even the thought of losing you is worse than death, worse than the thousands of torments I am willing to suffer for you.

My love, even the victories of Kings had no glory if they were not for love. While I am just a common man, my love for you is the same as the love of the great Kings for their land, of the priest for his pupil, of God for his children, of the air and the sky, of the wind and the mountains, of the land with its soil, of the river with its shore: in every form of nature my love resides, and my heart longs for you. Even a glimpse of you fulfils my sacred wish of loving you. You are an angel whose smile can cause destruction of this world and re-creation of a better one. I can never be what you deserve but somewhere in a corner of this existent land, I'll love you truly, more than any other person could; I can promise you that. Maybe it is my destiny, to love you, and to perish loving you.

He folded the letter twice and put it in a clean envelope. It was as if a grand scroll had been prepared which carried the ancient destiny of an empire, the message of obliteration of an entire race; as if the hunger and silence of this performance of speech and words would bring about, a much related change as predicted, in a woman's heart too.

"There you go," said the young writer, without any expression on his face.

He was a boy, a normal boy, a smart boy. He handed the letter to another boy, around the same age. The recipient looked at the letter, the envelope to be precise, and expressed through his eyes myriads of extreme actions one might perform in the given state of excitement; but the restlessness was unable to replace the calm on his face.

"Oh! I hope this works!" he murmured. "I need this badly right now. I am going to get several prints of this, and give it to my friends too."

These words did not distract the writer from his gaze which was directed outside the window. But his sharp glance showed he had been listening to every word that the recipient said, but was far more interested in keeping his views to himself: far away from the perimeters of morals; the definitions of right and wrong; or any possible results that may arise out of his fruitful invention–anything of that sort. He was greatly enjoying his newly acquired status of being a source that provides the best of love letters. But the thing that interested Ayan was not the intention of those he represented, nor the association or popularity he enjoyed; he always felt challenged by the naive yet complicated situations he used to observe of the boys who sought his help.

The recipient, on the other hand, oblivious, was walking about wearing his cargoes, boyish charm and a blue tee. He started to flip through the books and papers that were kept on Ayan's study table. "So what's new?" he asked.

"Well, nothing as such," Ayan said, noticing carefully the recipient's movements from a distance. "Exams. What else!"

The recipient grinned, "Yeah, I don't know if I am going to pass this year!" he said, picking up every object, fumbling through papers until his eyes found some letters.

"Wow, who are these for?" he asked loudly, out of excitement. He picked up one of the letters and quickly started to examine it, curiously trying to find its applicability in his own situation.

"I wrote that for someone else," Ayan said. "Look if you need another letter, I will write you one, or two, or as many as you want."

He was a little alerted by the sudden intrusion into his private territory by the recipient; but his alertness showed only through his eyes and voice. Perhaps he understood that the reason behind the recipient's sudden invasion was not the contents of the letter, but was aimed to unconsciously notice the nature of its preciousness to Ayan. But without any response by Ayan, who sat still, the recipient was forced to calmly surrender. He kept the letters back and sat on the chair that was stationed next to the table.

"So, where's Mezz?" He asked, finding it obligatory at this point to start some sort of conversation.

"I don't know. At his place."

"Anyway, I should head home. My tuitions ended an hour ago." The recipient winked and left.

Ayan stood up in relief, and threw himself on the chair where the recipient had sat a few moments ago. In silence, he took the letter which had already been unfolded by alien hands and read what was written at the top: 17th August, 2004.

This wasn't the first letter Ayan had written to this girl; it was one of the many letters he had written since he saw her at an International Convention held in his school on 26 January 2004. Although the girl was not a participant in any event that required some sort of intellectual display, which normally would have impressed or caught Ayan's eyes, not that that frequently happened with him, nor had he had ever fallen prey to a girl solely because of her smartness. Since it happened with this girl, it was impossible to deduce any intelligible reason behind the sudden-acquired attraction of the boy. Thenceforth, there wasn't a single moment in the boy's life that didn't have her thought, and he often cursed himself for it. He remembered her clearly from the time he saw her: from the colour of her clothes to the expressions on her face; the entire sequence, like a film was recorded in his mind.

He looked at the bunch of letters, all of them left in chaos, devoid of a position, an identity, and a character. These letters, as he knew, had no destiny, for a letter through a journey of transportation meets its desired eyes; and Ayan, at this moment, had no idea about the present that might, in a fully conscious state, influence the destiny of these letters. Of course he believed he was in love, but he had already been in something very close to love twice before.

His previous love-encounters, although one-sided, had had an enormous effect on his mind, nearly uprooting every hope that exists in a juvenile's mind, to seek love or to be in love. In Ayan's first love-encounter, when he was fourteen, he crafted a magnificent plan to win over the girl, but unfortunately, it worked against him at the end. He met two of her lovers – two amongst the many, who were superior in virtues such as power and wealth, and promised them the attention of the girl. He gained full material pleasures from the first lover and complete hegemonic domination over his peers under the company of the second. And lastly, he promised the girl safety from every boy who might trouble her in as well as outside the school, using the powers he had just recently hired, thus proving himself to be her hero. But things got out of his hands, and he had to lose all the three people.

His second love-encounter, which happened when he was fifteen, was much more intense and impacting than the previous one. It comprised of desperate attempts to prove to his friends how great and pure his love was; and in these efforts, he went to the limit of sitting under the sun on a boulder that was kept close to her house. Soon, it was destroyed too, after a little threat was raised by an unknown family member of the girl. He experienced his love evaporate in a second, for fear of being beaten up or the possibility of this whole affair reaching his family. What truly bothered him strongly after these events was the realization that he had never actually been in love, but had been under the spell of its illusions.

It was a conversation, when Ayan was thirteen, which had planted the foundation of the very first thought, the very first idea, and the very first definition of love in his mind. It was not the conversation that he remembered, but the outcome of it: a very simple thought which was expressed by the speaker, an older boy, who was reciting an anecdote about his own experience with a girl he had met the previous night. In his narration he told Ayan that he was willing to spend his entire life with that girl even if the condition was to remove every possibility of ever having sex. Such an idea immediately and effectively moulded itself in Ayan's mind as the definition of true love. From that point on, love to this young boy strictly meant putting it through this question – "Can I spend my entire life with this girl without wanting to have sex with her?"

And that was Ayan's first perception of true love at the age of thirteen, in the year 2000.

He looked at the letters and started reading them one by one.

21 February, 2004

Dearest,

Truly speaking, I can't think of a word right now. I have been thinking about what to say, writing it, and then re-writing it. I played my violin today. It has been long since I touched it. It had dust residing over it, somewhat undermining its beauty. My violin looked older to me, just casting a dim image of how life goes on; how every beautiful thing one day becomes dull but never loses the beauty of the nature of its function. I fell in love with it again, the moment I played it. It is the same with humans – each one of them being a victim of an individuality they have gained. How strange it is not to realize who we are and to postpone the answer by saying 'we are confused' every time! I simply ask– "are we?"

I wonder sometimes- how can impossibility take over our lives? How do we choose to forget emotions so often when we still silently remember them and cry over them? How could we believe that heaven is the end to all our good deeds and still call ourselves fairly good men?

04 March, 2004

Dearest,

When we say we love someone, we dehumanize love's true meaning, because we want that someone, and in that want is hidden a feeling unknown to us. To every person, love means a different thing. It serves as a reliever of pain to some, to others it's a joy, to some it's sexual in nature, to some it's lifelong companionship, the purposes keep changing. It could be anything to a person but if it's not beautiful, it isn't love. History speaks about love through several stories, great love stories of how a person waited his entire life to be with his or her love. I have read love letters written by many great men but I can never be like them. But I am sure about one thing: even if my love for you might not be strong enough to create history, or to ever prove its existence, it is still something I will believe in forever. Beneath every feeling there is a longing; a resolution left incomplete; and in every sound of our soul there is a truth which is seldom heard by our own mind. We are humans. We love to define ourselves, and then we defy ourselves with tears in our emptiest moments of loneliness. I am hearing this beautiful song, and it makes me sad. Suddenly words like 'beautiful', 'your presence', 'your touch' make me smile and shed a tear. I wish I could tell you someday how much I love you, and how much your absence has left me a living dead; how I hope that you always smile with that angelic face, with your lips retaining its cherry red colour and your eyes filled with the limitless innocence only God has known. I wish I could tell you how sad I feel sometimes; and how much I miss you in every single moment, for I fear it could be my last. I love you, my angel, and in this love, I have found my life; I have found the profoundest of truths:

that to love you is why I was created, and to have you will be the end of my life.

23 March, 2004

Love,

It's so little of me, in the form of my writings, to address the love I have for you, the mystery of which passes through the immeasurable heights of mountains and the unfathomable depths of oceans, through the light and darkness of nature, resulting in the belief of something unknown. It's only you I think about in the glimpse I share with the night, hopelessly ceasing to accept how unlucky I am. Is it fate or a test; that I can't meet the destiny whose craving has altered every other reality I once favored?

I sit here alone, vaguely listening to your voice dissolving gradually from my mind. I can never write fully in words what you mean to me, and that is the reason why the number of these letters will count to uncountable. Every word in my heart is dressed up in the hope of attracting your eyes, I feel a selfish craving of wanting you. Is it helpful? It is surely surprising. Maybe I have learnt the impossible now: that loving can be the destiny of many, but for some just the embrace of it is an experience of such value that meanings of their entire lives change.

What is beauty? Is it a far reaching notion that explains what could never be explained in words? Like sights of beauty that have in them: stillness; a thrill of containing what a mind is unwilling to absorb; an escape from the very grounds upon which a human stands, of thought; or an actual embrace of reality? Of goodness? Or perspectives! I seem to have lost my focus, which, with the combined force of nature and the universe, is directed upon you. My love, many a time I have dissolved myself into the vicissitudes of impossibility, gaining insights, and finding some sort of sense in them, but whenever I contemplate your existence in my life, I become a plain lover.

My dear love, I do not value tears highly, but the only language my love speaks is somehow of tears.

He kept the letters down and took a deep breath, looking at the pile of letters kept inside several files. He had lost count after they crossed fifty. He had turned seventeen now, on 21st June 2004, and the year 2005 was not far away.

Chapter - 2

As Ayan's eyes observed, in front of him at a distance stood a giant stage, almost seeming to engulf every single person who was positioned near it. He was amused by the blinding lights that blinked intermittently; the roars of the front-man of the music group, securing a safe place for himself in the animal kingdom; the sight of guitar players enjoying the sight of the many girls in the crowd who were pitching in with their own glass-breaking sounds; the front row collaborating with whatever the vocalist of the music group asked them to do, for example, to bang their heads, to start jumping, to sit down, to take their lighters out which was silly to ask of schoolchildren.

The rock show marked the ending of the the school function, which was named after an ancient mythical monster that bore no relation to the nature of the event. The organizers after having failed to find any relation between the two, came up with the idea that the name represented the grandness of the event, its monstrous size to be precise. Far away from these mysteries, these observations and the herd, two boys were sitting on another stage, which was built of bricks and concrete and marble, the stage upon which were conducted the morning prayers, the daily announcements, speeches, thoughts of the day, unlike the stage on which the rock band was currently performing, situated on the school's football ground. Ayan watched the show from the maintained distance; his eyes, unwilling to submit to the music or the commands of the musicians. He kept quiet for some time, then he asked the boy sitting next to him: "So, how does one become famous, Mezz?"

Mezz, whose attention the melodramatic musicians had failed to hold, was willing to answer anything at that moment, which would firstly, start a healthy conversation; and secondly, give him a chance to spread his ideologies.

He looked at Ayan and replied, "One either has to be a king or a fool to become famous; and you and I my friend, are neither." He paused. "If a wise man ever imitates a fool, he can be nothing but a disappointment; if a fool imitates a wise man, he becomes the butt of jokes."

"How do we know who is the King and who is the

Fool?" Ayan asked, pondering on his words.

"Well, the king is the most desirable man for women," Mezz said.

"Take a look around and you will find that while the Kings may be two and three only, the fools are in large numbers; they find each other easily and live in herds; they are bull-necked giants who are ready to fight even if one of them is challenged by the rival fools," he continued, "Fools are those who when talking to women, laugh maniacally; talk at an extremely higher pitch than their normal tone, which is out of excitement or maybe instincts! They portray themselves as no less than the descendants of Hercules; actually, they emphasize on that." By this time, Ayan was chuckling.

"They are those who stare into the eyes of girls, waiting for them to laugh at every stupid thing that comes out of their mouth, right after which they shoot another offspring of that joke and burst out laughing themselves."

"Come on, now!" Ayan said, "But girls do laugh at their jokes."

"And therefore, the conclusion that girls love kings and the fools." Mezz said, emphatically, "And let history be a witness to this fact."

"So who are we?" Ayan asked after a pause.

"We are wise men, Ayan," Mezz answered. "We are the councilmen of the kings who fill their minds with ideas of world domination, and send them to war while we sleep with their countless wives." He lay on his back and smiled.

"Kings are the most crippled beings, they are not like fools: a fool is one who thinks he is smart, and therefore is never unhappy. He is incorrigible. A fool is the audience of a smart man. On the other hand, kings know that they need the assistance of smart men, and that is what makes them incomplete."

"But what about the virtuous kings?" Ayan asked.

"You mean Plato's philosopher king? There are always exceptions, Ayan. In everything that I say there is an exception; against everything that is ever said by a man in this world stands an exception. We philosophize keeping the ninety-nine percent of people in our minds, and chuck that exception-making one percent out, to which as I understand, the philosopher himself belongs. It is human tendency to believe supremely in what is unreal and forget what really is unforgettable," Mezz said.

He looked at Ayan realizing that he was lying down beside him too.

"And what becomes of the wise?" Ayan questioned further.

"A wise man that turns smart becomes rich; and a wise man that remains wise becomes obscurely great," Mezz replied, looking at the sky.

"Like Spinoza?" Ayan asked.

"Like Spinoza," Mezz affirmed, "and every other philosopher."

They both chuckled, and stayed quiet for a while.

"So, who's the most stupid?" Ayan finally asked.

"Girls, of course," Mezz answered mockingly.

Ayan laughed and stood up. "Let's leave now. And hey, where's that new girl you were making out with, behind that bus?" he said pointing to the school-bus which was parked peacefully in a corner, far away from the rock show, in darkness.

"Oh yes, I completely forgot about her, and her name. She must be there, stuck in the middle of the guys," Mezz said, pointing towards the stage where the show was still going on. He stood still for a moment. "Ah! F…her, let's go!"

Both of them walked towards the exit gate of their school, which was naturally packed with people entering and leaving. They somehow made their way out and away from the noises of chattering, things cracking and dropping, and all sorts of sounds, finally entering the realm of normality as they walked down the street to their homes.

"Anyway, I forgot to tell you. I met that guy: Sara's boyfriend," Mezz said, referring to the girl from Ayan's letters.

"What is he like?" Ayan asked.

"A complete blockhead!" Mezz said. "We waited fifteen minutes outside his house because he was putting on make-up or something." Ayan smirked but still remained quiet.

"They will break-up, that's for sure," Mezz added.

Ayan kept himself away from any such interpretations for mainly two reasons: first, he had never pictured himself in a relationship with Sara, and therefore any such ideas didn't interest or amuse him at all; second, he firmly believed that she wasn't ready to be introduced to the kind of love he had to offer. It may surprise her, and intrigue her, after all who doesn't love the idea of true love; but he believed that at their age, a relationship was more inclined towards following the common pattern of relationships.

Apart from that, he had also learned that people wanted to be in a relationship for many other reasons than just love, stretching from societal acceptance to carnal needs. Having heard about her past amorous experiences, he had figured out that her idea of love was the completion of the circle of her luxurious wants, in which having a boyfriend was an essential feature. He believed that she had no idea what love was, and if he gave her those letters, she would not be able to understand his feelings. He knew that she would admire every word written in them, but it would be only because every person dreams about such romantic gestures.

Ayan's love was more like a fairy-tale love at this moment; it had no soul but it had a story. He had decided to wait for her to go to college, to be free from the parenting bonds and chains and hands that had been protecting her from all the evils of the world. He wanted her to grow up and see the true nature of this world that knows only truth and no fairy tales or dreams. And because of such assumptions, the letters had finally gained a destiny. Although written a long time before their journey, they served to be the testimony of his love.

"So, what's your plan?" Mezz asked.

"What can I do?" Ayan asked, rhetorically. "I can't break them up, and if it does happen naturally, let's say tomorrow, how is it any good for me? The concept of love in her mind is absolutely worthless to pursue. On the contrary, it is a mockery. We make fun of these things all the time, and now you expect me to be a part of it?" He paused for a while.

"Even if I get to be with her, I have nothing, dude. People need money. Let's assume she's very understanding too, but one still needs money. I don't have a car to take her on dates. I can't call her, talk to her all night because I don't have a rich dad to pay my bills. And to be honest, even if I had that kind of money I'd probably spend it on books instead of some stupid invention to ... up my time! Whatever the truth be, I love this girl, and I can wait, Mezz. I don't want to have her at a time when she, out of immaturity, may find it plausible to leave me. I would prefer to have her when I can have her completely. I can wait." Ayan said.

"And what if you have underestimated her? What if she doesn't care about all of this ?" Mezz asked.

"Really? After all we know about her? You believe that?"

"No, I am just messing with you," Mezz said. "I hate attractive women. An attractive woman even if completely purposeless, unknowingly possesses the power to change the destiny of many, many men."

They both walked quietly after that; both of them sinking into their own thoughts. It was hard, in fact, impossible, to choose the smarter lad out of the two, for they both had their own distinct gifts.

Ayan had the gift of beautiful powers of observation

while Mezz had the gift of verbal speech or as some might say–manipulation. It was not surprising. The notoriety Mezz had gained over the years as his anecdotes spread through the minds and mouths of young men–too many of which were rumours, simply fictional inventions of his followers; some were exaggerations but some were awfully true. He had the image of a lady's man, not that he had had countless sexual encounters or escapades that made him such an intriguing character among his fellow-men. He was well-known for his unbelievable quests. One of Mezz's many stories narrated how he once courted six girls at the same time. They were all best friends and never talked to any guy, in fact any other person out of their group. Such were the types of challenges that inspired him and made his name famous in different schools. Mezz had a way of speaking (so he believed) that could turn a man against his own brother, and he never cared to throw away such a chance, which was the reason for his infamy. His methods of testing human nature by exposing it to chaos, to destruction, led him to want to learn the true nature of man, hiding underneath all his masks.

21 December, 2004

Dearest,
Sometimes hope seems to be the worst thing, hope to find the thing you've made your peace with. Even a glimpse of you takes my wretched life to a new wretchedness; and knowing that I am a man of words, not action, your sight makes me write the saddest things ever written. What one loves

has the tendency to become what one wants the most; and it increases one's expectations, respect, and value for it. My love for you has been more sacred than anything except for my craving for knowledge, but maybe the desire is dead now. You're no more a feeling or a part in me which is incomplete, instead you're the reason I want to live for and take responsibility–a love that has helped me to figure out one of the greatest truths of my life: loving someone deeply or truly is not love but to make yourself worthy of that love, is love.

Chapter – 3

At the time Ayan and Mezz were growing up together, they had no similarities. One thing that they both had programmed in them was the common hatred for the company of other people and as they grew up, they developed certain mechanisms on how to deal with it. Ayan became peculiarly interested in understanding the human mind and its connection with emotions, fears, wants, desires, needs, ends; categorizing human minds into classes and, therefore dwelling into history, and choosing from it the men he wanted to have a dialogue with. He read about philosophers all day, and finally restricted himself to

Metaphysics, Political thought, and Literature. But he was a growing boy, which was evident in the notes he made in his diary: about the meaning of life, world, human bonding, love and society.

When he was fifteen he wrote about destiny: that every person is born with one, and his every step should be towards its fulfillment. He wrote: *And recognizing your destiny will come naturally by letting your conscience decide for you.* To him the world was like a map, except it was not a map of the world at all. He thought: *it is every man walking towards his destiny like walking down a one–way street, and the roads crossing each other are the indications where you might meet other people: they were the spots where stories (individuals) met and destinies of two, or three, or more people, merged for sometime–but all relationships must end and you shall walk individually as focused and refined as you had started.*

He strongly maintained the idea of individuality in this mind, and to live it, he would often take walks alone at night. As more time passed, he fell in love with the world, with each place that he had visited. He fell in love with the moments that he had shared with a place, as if the buildings and the architectural erections somehow gave a meaning to his very existence; as if there had been an association beyond time between him and these pieces of land. But he never felt any connection with nature, as a result of which, he had no love or fondness for nature at all. This was the time when he worked very hard and made two of the greatest intellectual discoveries of his life: the pure concepts and the true nature of thought.

He simply wrote down the things that have influenced humans throughout the ages, such as love, music, literature, history, painting, friendship, and more; discarding industrial growth, mechanical developments, and biological discoveries. He maintained that true human happiness, which is divine peace, rested in the following things, and no materialistic pleasure could replace or even come close to the purity of such concepts. And therefore he called them pure concepts as they linked with the universal soul of a person rather than the mind, which was the product of the age it belonged to.

At seventeen, Ayan renounced all the material pleasures; he had closed the doors to all the wants that haunted other children of his age: clothes, gadgets, cars, or girls. He sought happiness in only one thing, and that was humour, and those possessing humour were the only people he liked to converse with. Later on, he added one more concept to his list of pure concepts: war. After reading about wars at great length, he believed that: Strife is in the very nature of human soul, just as domination, greed, selfishness, and power. He was moved deeply by German philosophy and the sounds of glory; tales of great wars and heroes. He started reading about Napoleon, the World wars, Alexander, the siege of Troy, and various historical stories that filled his mind with juvenile fantasies and theoretical definitions of honour and manhood. But violence for him did not become the means to achieve peace. He maintained that war in itself was the combination of all pure concepts. He was so impressed by the idea of war that he often used to write stories about fictional warriors, their sacrifices, and their grand conquests; but all of this never distracted him from the other pure concepts, and while he sought detachment from worldly pleasures, the pure concepts continued to serve him in the most beautiful manner.

He played the guitar and the violin almost like a virtuoso. He practiced music at two or three in the morning, sometimes even outside his house in the park, or any place that suited his inspiration at that given moment. He didn't play a piece of music that was composed by some other musician. He maintained that, the music that has already been played is only meant to be cherished by listening; therefore since the beginning of his self-restricted musical career, he only played his own music.

The other intellectual discovery of his was the true nature thought, which according to him meant: *the pure thought that arises out of a man's reason and logic, rather than an alien influence.* It was something he respected and sought the most in people, although he hadn't met any person, other than the deceased men through their books, and Mezz, who possessed it. To him it wasn't wisdom, even though very closely related to it: *True nature thought is the first thought as a response to an external, intellectual stimulus, forcing one to emerge with a reaction, a solution, a comment, a perspective, a question, an idea, a notion, disagreement, almost everything, except for the dull nod. It is destroyed instantly when a person picks up a book to read; in the very moment when a person submits his reason and logic and gives in to what others have to say, in the following of men, in blind admiration.* Such were the early writings of Ayan, apart from the letters.

As the year 2004 approached its end, Ayan was haunted by a problem–his classmates, whom he had always considered as acquaintances, suddenly resorted to unreasonable suggestions and demands that he act in order to have Sara as his lover, which confused and surprised him. He listened to their mindless, and sometimes well planned strategies to court her: some of them being: 'stopping her in the middle of the road when she is coming back from school, and talking to her openly about his feelings'; others ranged from 'taking the assistance of a mutual friend' to 'taking the assistance of a female friend who would contact her and give her the love letters'.

The reason why such suggestions and plans had suddenly become such a confusing dilemma for Ayan was the constant fear of losing her completely. It didn't mean that he feared the very obvious possibility that she might fall in love with another man; of course, he was well aware of that eventuality. He believed that if such a thing were to happen and if their love could be stronger or even more sacred than his or what he had envisioned in his mind, then there would be no sense in taking any step further. What he truly feared was his inability to find out her whereabouts once she left the school; he had no idea about her plans, nor did they have any mutual friend.

27 December, 2005

Dearest,

I wonder what would have happened if I had missed the most important discovery of my life–the love for you.

I sit here, imagining you as the most immaculate creation ever made in the entire course of history. Should I express my love for you in the most articulate speech ever made, I would fail every time to explain how much beauty even a slight glimpse of you has in words that would be impossible for me to write down. In simple words, I love you. I love you every single moment; I love you in every word which speaks of love; I love you in the notes of music; and I love you even more when I don't want to.

Chapter - 4

Ayan was sitting in his room with a book between his hands, going through excerpts of writings and flipping through pages as if he was searching for a passage, at which point, he heard the voice of his uncle calling his name to which he replied by not replying at all. Ayan's uncle called his name only when his friends came to visit. He lived in the house of his late grandfather, whom he had never met but had heard stories of: great Indian tales of hunting, and ghosts-catching, and taming wild animals: the fearless man that the entire town respected and feared at the same time, the one who had the sinister looking moustache that never, even for a second, he forgot to twist and twirl, even when the furious bandits from the ominous valley approached the town with guns. He waited for them alone in the darkness, clad in a black silk shawl in the cold winter breeze, ready to face anything. But such were not the stories of his Grandfather. On the contrary, he had never fully heard a story about anyone: his grandfather, father, or his mother. He knew the part where his father was kicked out of the house by his grandfather, and that later, he married another woman who bore him three children: two boys and a girl. Also in accordance with what he was told, his mother died when he was two years old.

He was brought up by his uncle, who took utmost care of him, showering his affection and giving him right knowledge of the world, choosing carefully the company of friends when he was young, and leading him to mingle and grow up with Mezz, who now stood at the door of Ayan's room.

"We have to go. Get up!" Mezz said.

"Where to?" Ayan asked, picking himself up in a second.

"To the market. My dad had ordered some books. Have to go pick them up."

When they were walking towards their destination, Ayan asked, "So, what's up?"

"Nothing!" Mezz said, looking lost.

"Why the sad face?" Ayan asked.

"Just this girl, man." Mezz replied.

"What girl?" Ayan asked.

"Okay," Mezz said, "try picturing this: take a character

who is not even remotely interested in art, development of taste, politics; I mean anything that gives me an opportunity to impress her. Now I am trying to court this chick here. So the list of topics goes like this: music, yes, she likes listening to music but whatever is playing on the radio. She is not very impressed by books, or literature, finds history boring, although she is very fond of bollywood flicks, whose names would make you puke. So finally I asked her views about visual art?" He paused, "She finds it pleasing to her eyes. Now what do you think of her?" Mezz asked Ayan.

"She is lame," Ayan said, without giving it a thought.

"Yes, exactly! That's what it looks like, but," he paused, "there is a but. Can you believe it?" He looked sharply at Ayan.

"The but is that she is not lame; she actually has a mildly functioning brain, because when I asked her what she thinks about certain normal, conversation-making topics such as love, or life, you know what I found? She has a self-made theory on every given thing, and not just blind bullshit that people are obsessed with relating themselves to. When you read this chick's answers, her ideologies, regardless of how lame or cool they may sound, make perfect sense in her frog-well world."

He continued, "I am not saying that I am impressed. I am surprised and greatly confused because I can't figure out a way to court her. I am calling her the uninterested science." He took another pause, investing the carefully chosen time to look for the book-shop, as they stood in the midst of the market now, which gave Ayan the opportunity to ask him the only thing that had intrigued him throughout this conversation: "So, she possesses true nature thought?"

"Well," Mezz said, "not exactly true nature thought, they are more like cartoon drawings of a four year old, but very amusing. Like a really creative kid who is very lazy to explore something new."

"Let me think," Ayan said. "Your problem is not her personality. From the beginning you were subconsciously expecting something in her that will amuse you, something, anything, to give you a reason to court her. And when you found these stupid ideologies, you found your something, and instead of understanding this simple truth that she is not worth it, which might repel you even more, you chose to relate it with something very close to true nature thought." He noticed that Mezz was carefully listening to him.

"Now, I will tell you the problems. Your first problem is her standard. Obviously as she hasn't ever given any priority to quality, her idea of love could very much involve a simple guy, who watches lame movies and believes in hardcore biking, and all that crap; on the other hand, you have a standard, about which she doesn't care."

"So if you want to woo her, you will have to be a simple guy, and want what simple guys want, and do what simple guys do."

"I don't know what they want," Mezz said, "but I do know what they do: they dream and they waste their time."

Ayan chuckled, "Your second problem is that it has

become a matter of your ego now. Your third problem is that you're unable to locate a loophole in her system of thought."

After picking up the books, they both decided to eat something, and marched in the direction of the nearest Coffee shop.

"You know what you can do; you can try being her psychologist," Ayan suggested.

"That's exactly what I have been doing," Mezz replied.

"What's her name?"

"Crash. Crash boomerang"

"How many mails or messages have you exchanged with this chick?" Ayan asked.

"Around three hundred."

"So you already knew all the things that I said!"

"Of course I did!" Mezz replied.

"What's the catch then? These messages are above five hundred words each, aren't they?" Ayan asked.

Mezz nodded.

"So it really is true nature thought then, isn't it?"

"Sort of," Mezz said, partly agreeing.

"So you are also saying that this girl is smart?"

"Not smart, but really bright." Mezz paused for a moment, after which he murmured: "Exception, huh? But your part is true too; she does have this self image which often stops her from doing what she wants to." Mezz said, deeply engrossed in thought.

"So, are you in love with this chick?"

"No!" Mezz exclaimed.

"Well, three hundred ...ing mails is a disturbing thought, and a little too much unlike Mezz."

"No, no, no, no, no, no!" Mezz said, with every following monosyllable descending in volume, the last one becoming merely a whisper. They had reached the coffee shop.

"Love," Mezz said, "is the weak man's assumption to acquire or ascertain happiness, or inner peace." He pulled up a chair outside the coffee shop, which was an extension of the store.

"An idea becomes what people make it, Ayan. And I don't care about the true nature of love; it doesn't exist in this world, and to me it doesn't make sense. It's logically inept and foolish."

They both sat in positions which if viewed from above, made the circular table look like a round clock with Ayan and Mezz, sitting at 2 and 6 o'clock respectively.

"Think of it practically, what is the most fickle thing in this world?" Mezz asked.

"What?" Ayan threw the question back at him.

"The human mind," Mezz said. "It's the most fickle thing in this world. A person never knows what he truly wants, but desires everything; and in all of this, what should be my approach; when I know that my mind is constantly wandering, betraying my previous resolutions, and dragging me into wanting these new things that I haven't a clue about; when terms like the next best thing and cool have taken over the world."

"The entire idea of love has transformed into dating,

and the literal meaning of relationship has changed into countless relationship statuses; out of which, being single is a stigma for a guy and an 'I am available' sign for a girl. We are slaves to our new industrial rulers, who rule our minds with televisions and advertisements and sales and with the next best thing. They convince us of the next definition to become cool. I ask, what is this definition of 'being cool'? Being fooled?"

"Now, in all of these trends," Mezz said, "all of these patterns, what must be done? What should I do to keep my mind focused, and not be one among the crowds, and not be a fucking consumer? I need to exercise self-control, right? I have to control my thoughts, keep my mind away from the timely evaporating temptations that look like fucking gold. But then hey! What do I do? I fall in love and have a girlfriend; and you know what that means? I have another mind now, another most fickle thing in the world to whom I have given the control of my happiness. Now, not only do I have to control my mind and take my own responsibility to be truly, consciously awake, and make the right decisions, but I have to make sure that the other mind I have conjoined my life with, understands this too." He stopped and rested his back on the chair with a magnanimous smile.

"After this, you get the rest of the picture: you are spending the rest of your life explaining, controlling, especially fixing what is messed up in her life from her past, trying to make permanent amendments so she doesn't have to go through those kind of troubles again. You waste your entire time living happily in the hope that she is now free and enlightened by the knowledge and great wisdom you have bestowed upon her; that she would be unaffected by the next big thing: which in this case is symbolic of guys with big cars and cash." He took a sip from the coffee mug.

It had been placed in front of him some three minutes ago, by a young man who worked at that coffee store and seemed intrigued by the bits of Mezz's conversation that fell into his ears, distracting him from wherever his mind was hovering.

"You were right that day: Love is the luxury of the rich," Mezz said.

"So, what is your grand solution?" Ayan asked after a second's thought.

"Why do I care? I'll tell you what I want," he said and leaned forward.

"I want a good time.I don't want to change someone's life, or control someone. If you like someone else and think your life would be better off with him, then you have my blessings. " He waved his hands.

"At least I never act for selfish reasons in a relationship, like every guy who is in love tells his girl-friend thousands of scary stories and facts about how evil other guys are, and how they start with friendship but end up hitting on you. A girl never realizes that he is not doing it to warn her against those type of guys, but because, he has an inferiority complex. Moreover he doesn't trust her a bit, and hence is using fear as a weapon, so that whenever she meets a guy, she is already so scared from the stories she has heard that it's in her mind to avoid even talking to him."

"On the contrary, I tell girls to go out and have a good time. I tell them that the only exception is that there are no exceptions. You go party, befriend whomever you want to. I mean, I trust your judgment; you don't need to be told what to do! I am selfless. You know what, I am the angel here," Mezz said, smiling mischievously.

"You never stop them from doing anything because you want them to make mistakes. It gives you reasons to break up with them, and also after you have broken up with them, there is no guilt," Ayan said, chuckling.

They both stayed quiet for a while, for the first time concentrating on the design of the coffee mugs, inducing from them maximum heat through their palms by feeling them all around to ward off December cold in New Delhi. They looked around and spotted a young girl wearing a fairly short dress, sitting inside the coffee shop. Mezz coughed twice and Ayan thought about Sara.

"So what did you think?" Mezz asked, finally breaking the silence.

"About what?" Ayan asked.

"About all the brilliant suggestions you have been getting to approach Sara," he said laughing.

Ayan responded by shaking his head in wonder.

"That friend of yours, Aman, is really crazy," Ayan said. "You know what he told me to do? He told me to go and stop her in the middle of the road, and do whatever I needed to. So I asked him, what about the people around? I can't just forcibly stop a girl in the middle of a road to talk to her! He said, Don't worry; we'll block the traffic for as long as you want."

"I mean, can you f…believe that? Who is he?"

Mezz was laughing loudly. "That guy has got some big connections. He literally knows everybody..." Before Mezz could finish the sentence, he noticed Ayan's frozen expression.

"Mezz, there's Sara!" he murmured.

"Where?" Mezz asked. "On your right; on the other side of the road." Ayan said, hardly moving his lips as he spoke.

Mezz looked and spotted the tall leggy girl in a tweed coat, accompanied by another girl.

"Yeah," Mezz said looking at them, "and it's a lovely suit she is wearing!"

"What should we do?" Ayan asked.

"What do you mean: what should we do?" Mezz said in a mocking tone. "You've got a chance to look at her, so have a good look for God's sake!"

Ayan was terrified, and his mind simply stopped working. He sat there with immense fear in his heart, so much fear that he wanted to run away without any explanation or cause. In this moment, there wasn't any sense in him to understand that he had a body, an obligation to breathe, to sustain as a legitimate part of society. He looked at her hesitatingly, getting scared by the possibility that she might catch him looking at her, while she stood far away to even notice such a daring act being executed by his scared eyes. But unfortunately she did, and it was in fact her friend who caught Sara's hand and pointed towards them. "Is that chick pointing at us?" Mezz asked.

"Holy shit, look straight!" Ayan said, loudly. "What the fuck was that? Why the hell was she pointing at us?"

Mezz looked at the girls completely confused.

"How the hell would I know; and it's not us, it's you. You're the one who is in love with her!"

Mezz turned his head and found that the girl with Sara, the same girl who was pointing them out a few moments ago, had taken her phone out and was calling somebody. "Okay, that friend of hers is calling someone; do you think we are in trouble?" Mezz asked.

"Let's get out of here; my mind is not working," Ayan said, grabbing the books that were kept on the table. They both stood up and started to walk away. "What the hell was that?" Mezz asked, jumping from one spot to another, looking at Ayan, who at this moment, was simply walking as fast as he could, deeply engrossed as if he had witnessed a catastrophe of some sort.

"She knows! Who could have thought that?" By this time, it was confirmed that Mezz was speaking to himself and his mind was occupied in breaking down the entire course of this event mathematically, starting from all the people who knew about this, and from them to those who had or could possibly gain access to Sara.

"Who could have told her?" Mezz asked. "And it wasn't Sara but her friend who pointed towards you, which means that she knew how you look, and Sara had only heard of you. Did that chick look familiar to you?" And he submitted himself into solving another mystery. Both of them walked at a much faster pace and took all the shortcuts, reaching Ayan's house as quickly as possible. After entering his room, for the first time after the incident they breathed easy. Ayan chose his couch and threw himself on it, with an expression of shock still lingering on his face, while whereas Mezz walked around mumbling equations and shooting theories.

"Come on, what do you think? Ayan, what are you thinking?" He sat beside him.

"I love her," Ayan mumbled.

"What?"

"I love her." His voice strengthened this time. "She was right in front of me; I am no longer in doubt or anything. I love this girl more than my life." Ayan stood up with an expression of self-pity. "What have I been doing? Wasting all this time away."

"Now suddenly you think you should have dated her?" Mezz asked in confusion.

Ayan sat down again with his head sinking beneath his hands.

"Not dated, but at least talked to her, I should have told her." he said.

"She knows," Mezz said.

"From somebody else, and I don't even know what definition of my love she is carrying in her head." He paused, "It's about how much I love her; she may not know anything that I feel." He paused and looked into Mezz's eyes. "In that moment, I truly felt something," he said. "I knew that I can die for this girl."

After that moment, Mezz didn't say a word; it was not in Ayan's speech, nor the degree of assurance his words carried, it was in his eyes where he could see a strange amount of seriousness; a very devoted dedication that calmed Mezz down. "So how are we doing this?" Mezz asked.

"I'll have to do it myself," Ayan said. "Certainly we can't trust anyone around us."

"Schools are off right now," Mezz said, "and I think it's directly going to be pre-boards and no school now; at least for students."

"What about her house? We can fix something there, can't we?" Ayan asked, thinking deeply.

"She lives far away," Mezz emphasized. "And what are we going to do; stalk her? Wait outside her house to see when she comes out alone?"

"What about coaching centers? Tuitions?" Ayan asked.

"I don't know, but I guess I can find out." Mezz suggested.

"No finding out with someone's help; no more involving anyone now. Screw the home thing. School it is," Ayan said.

"But the pre-boards are not too far away; it's not a good time," Mezz said.

"I am just giving her those letters, and not asking her

to make a decision; not asking her for anything," Ayan said defending his plan.

"True!" Mezz said. "But think: If you are doing it, then do it completely, for the sake of your love. At least give her the time to read them and understand them and who knows she might really want to talk to you after that."

"But I don't want any of that, and nor do I expect any such thing to happen," Ayan argued.

"Dude, for once, think positively. You could be her friend. No one's asking you to f… her, or be her boyfriend," Mezz said angrily.

"So after the boards?" Ayan said.

"Of course not, we'll find out which college she joins," Mezz said in a casual manner.

"You think so?" He looked at Mezz in amazement. "None of us is that useless." Ayan said.

29 December, 2004

Dearest,

There is subtlety in my life tonight. I get a feeling that brings me closer to words like death, surrender, sorrow, and pity. But then I wonder about God's work of creating me, to make me who I am, and I have no answer; but the answer simply can't be the words that I am thinking. It is a moment in which angels smile, for they know the answer, and even when they love you they don't whisper it in your ears, or let you know in your dreams. They want you to wait and find out for yourself. I wonder sometimes: What is the fear of death? and how does it feel to face death? Is it calm? Is it similar to this moment?

Dear love, how strange it is, when all that I believed about love, in its utmost heroic sacrificing manner, gradually appears to be wrong. I believed a man's strength can always change the path of his thoughts, but the river that flows can never recite the story of the water it carries, and such is love: it doesn't depend upon the will of a man to overcome it, or defeat it. It defies strength, and hence to the greatest of men: love preaches all and teaches all; and like the water in a river, it speaks of immortality in a man; and just as water never sees the river it flows in, love never sees who the person is. This is the truth of my life. I can't escape from loving you, how hard I may try, I can't stop loving you. So I let the pain smother me and the incompetency torture me. How helpless I find myself tonight, for I am unable to write even the smallest part of what my heart wants to say to you!

Chapter - 5

Sara woke up with her eyes tightly shut, a usual expression of still wanting to sleep, or being astounded over the fact that it was a dream and not reality, where the handsome prince charming had ridden over from the other corner of the world just to find her, and their true love story was complete. She smiled after suddenly remembering the very tiny detail which made the day very special for her. She opened an eye and slid her right hand inside the massive formation of pillows scattered over the large bed. After the failed attempt, she opened both her eyes to see where her phone was lying, but without much effort, she gave up, sat there rubbing her eyes and yawning. She heard two knocks on her door and the voice of her father: "Happy birthday, my angel, are you up?"

"Yeah, dad." She smiled. It was the smile only a few people very close to her were familiar with. It was a smile that depicted true happiness. And the importance of this smile emerged only because of the lack of it. Sara didn't like smiling but she did smile a lot because she was a very simple person, and she never ever wanted to appear rude even to strangers. Her father entered the room, smiling. He hugged her, landed pecks on both the cheeks and asked: "What does my angel want for her birthday?"

"I want to go to Mumbai," she said in a demanding manner.

"I meant birthday present, Sara; don't you want something–like clothes, or..." He appeared to be lost for a moment trying to think of things she may desire.

"No." She said. "I already have everything I want; I want to go to Mumbai for my studies."

"What is there in Mumbai that isn't in Delhi?" Her father asked.

"Are you kidding me, dad?"

"Sara," he continued, "you want to study History. What's so advantageous about it in Mumbai that I should even consider this rant of yours? You can do that here in Delhi."
"Dad," she said in a protesting voice, "I wanna go, please! What are you afraid of? I am a big girl now, I can take care of myself. And I have so many friends there too," she said

as convincingly as she possibly could.

"So, is it about friendship?" Her father asked.

"No, I was just making a point that you don't have to worry about me being safe and all," she said.

Her father continued, "my point is: what's wrong with Delhi University? you will still have half of your friends around you, and your parents," he said and walked out of the room. Sara followed him.

"Dad, but I want to go away," she protested, "and not live in this house. I want to live alone and learn so many different things about life that I wouldn't if I stay in Delhi."

"Oh! gibberish," her father uttered with a grin.

"Stop using big words. It doesn't change that you're wrong," Sara said. Her father was laughing as he listened to her.

"Dad, please." She spotted her mother in the kitchen and ran towards her.

"Mom," she said, "please! make him understand. I want to go. What's so wrong about wanting to go to Mumbai?" She walked inside the kitchen and hugged her mother from behind. Her mother, at this moment was busy cooking. "Happy birthday!" She responded. "Look what I am cooking specially for you: all your favorite dishes!" she said.

"I am not staying; I have to go out with Trisha," Sara said.

"Right now? In the morning?" Her mother asked.

"Shouldn't you be happy about this: a morning party?" She said, looking for something to eat in the kitchen.

"I am not going in the night, which is wrong." She

stretched and whispered the last word. "I have to hang out with Trisha, and then there is this little get together of close friends at this small restaurant we have booked. Nothing like a party, since it's in the morning," she said, putting a chocolate cookie between her lips.

"You haven't even brushed your teeth." Her mother complained.

"On it, Mom," she said and moved jauntily, singing a song, in her tiny pink colored shorts, white tee, and designer slippers.

"And by the way, Dad, I am going to Mumbai as soon as my exams are over. I am going to stay at Neetu aunty's place and fill all the forms and everything from there. I have already talked to her about this and she is very excited about it. And yes! I also need your credit card for today," she said as she spotted her father in the living room reading the newspaper.

At eleven in the morning, she headed to Trisha's house in one of her father's cars. She wore a red tweed coat speckled with black dots, a short grey dress inside, black opaque stockings, black suede boots, and carried a black leather handbag. She never tried hard to decorate herself, but possessed such elegance that made others subconsciously dislike her, which made them consciously adore her. It was never her purpose to show off, to seek something as insignificant as attention. She was neither a sheep nor the shepherd. She took her phone out from the bag and positioned it very casually in front of her face like a book, holding it in her hand. The look on her face changed from the usually straight face to surprise, as the screen of her phone showed 15 unread messages. She quickly started to read them, and smiled after she read the first, blushed after the second, and blushed deeper and deeper as she continued to read them all. There was a constant smile on her face from this moment. She thought about the previous night's conversation with Nilay and the promise she had made to him. She was so much in love with him that she had planned her entire life with him: something she did with every boy she had been in a relationship with; but she believed Nilay was different, because he was mature, and had taught her all the good things that grown-ups do–smoking, hanging out till two in the morning with friends, partying, drinking, and having fun.

He had had many relationships before Sara, and this fact served as an assurance to her that she was, in some way, special and better. For her he was the complete painting of the juvenile idea of the perfect lover. Although he did have many problems too, problems that were not wholly hidden from Sara; for example: every time he talked about his past relationships, his voice changed, particularly when he talked about his former lover who had broken up with him, but she interpreted it in a personal competitive manner as the standard she had to achieve in order to become his 'cool girlfriend'. She would very attentively listen to everything about his former lover, so she would learn to prove herself a better companion, ignoring the simple possibility that he might still have romantic feelings for her. She never cared to study his voice or his reactions while he was narrating stories and anecdotes from the past. However, she did know the shorter and convincing version of the story: that they mutually broke up because his ex-girlfriend had to go abroad for her studies, but what she didn't know was the truth: that she had cheated on him, and when he found out, it was hard for him to count with how many boys!

She reached Trisha's house, and her father's driver drove the car back. She had already called Trisha from her phone to be ready. She rang the bell of the giant mansion. The front door opened and a house-maid peeped through it, quickly recognized Sara, smiled and headed back to inform Trisha. After a moment, a girl popped out from the same door, jumping excitedly. "Happy birthday!" She screamed and hugged Sara tightly.

"Thanks." Sara said, smiling.

"And oh my god!" Trisha exclaimed, "You look so pretty! Where did you get this coat from? Let me see." She checked the coat until she found her answer. "Oh my god! It's Chanel! Hot! And I love your dress too!"

Sara smiled some more, and asked: "Yeah, so how are we going?"

"Oh don't worry, *papa* is sending the car," she said. "And Nilay is going to be there. I talked to him a while ago; I even asked him whether he has bought you a birthday present," she said excitedly. "He told me that you are staying over at his place?"

"Yeah, I am unsure about that," Sara said. "What should

I do?" She had genuine anxiety in her voice.

"What, you don't know?" Trisha reacted in surprise. "I thought he said that you have promised him or something!"

"Yeah, I did." "But he was insisting, and I couldn't have said 'no' after knowing that he has come to Delhi only for my birthday." By this time, Trisha's car had finally arrived. They both got into it and headed to the destination–the little celebration.

"So what are you saying?" Trisha asked. "You don't wanna go to his place?"

"I don't know," Sara said in a confused manner. "I am not sure. If I go, I know something is going to happen, and I don't want to harm the relationship by doing anything too soon."

"What have you told your parents ?" Trisha asked.

"I have told them about the celebration only," Sara confessed.

"No night plans?"

"Nope," she replied, and appeared more and more worried as the car moved at a greater speed. "What should I do? you tell me," she asked Trisha.

"You can tell your parents that you are staying with me. I'll take care of everything," Trisha said.

"Not about my parents, Trisha; it is about Nilay!" Sara said in a tense manner. "What should I tell him to make him understand?"

"Just tell him what you told me," Trisha said. "I think he'll understand, I guess."

"He won't!" Sara murmured.

"You relax, okay!" Trisha said trying to comfort her. "It's your birthday today. I'll tell him that my mother has made birthday plans with both our families, and that's why you can't stay with him. How is that?"

Sara stayed quiet.

"I don't know," Sara said, unsure about what to do. "I really want to stay with him, but I don't know. I am confused." She looked sad.

"Just give it time," Trisha said. "Enjoy the party, and when you meet him, you will figure out what to do! After all, you have decided to go to Mumbai for him; I am pretty sure he understands how much you love him."

"Yeah, I hope so too," Sara said, relaxing a little. "I don't know if he will understand now after I have promised him. He's been sending me all these cute messages. He's come from Mumbai just for two days."

"Then stop thinking about it too much," Trisha said. "Forget it now. By the way, I forgot to tell you about..." And from that point, Trisha told her the story of the girl in their class, who secretly had affairs with many boys, but always pretended to be sexually innocent and morally chaste. Then she told Sara the story of the boy who was caught watching an adult film in the school's computer lab, at which they both laughed. And then the story of the gang battles of their schools, which Trisha took very seriously and Sara simply frowned upon. The car came to a smooth halt. They had reached their destination.

They got out of the car, and the driver drove it back. Sara looked at the building, which was a bar cum lounge cum disco cum whatever was profitable and in demand at the time.

"Come, let's go! The celebration is upstairs," Trisha said, moving towards the big wooden door which was the entrance to the place. Sara grabbed her hand and stopped her. "Just wait," she said. "One second, please!"

"What?" Trisha exclaimed. "It's freezing cold out here."

"I don't want to appear all excited," Sara explained. "I will be meeting him after two months. Let me just calm down, and also make up my mind on the staying-over-thing."

"Okay, seriously, what do you want, Sara?" Trisha asked.

Sara's face had turned red because of the cold.

"I am not yet ready for sex, Trisha." Sara finally shared what was going on her mind. "I love him so much; but my last relationship got ruined because of it. And I can't think of anything like that happening with Nilay. I haven't even moved to Mumbai yet." The tone of her voice changed from worried to sad.

"I can't," Sara said finally. "I will go for a drive, hang out with him in the evening, but at night I am coming back to my place." Before she could ask Trisha for her opinion, Trisha said: "Holy shit! It's him."

She grabbed Sara by her arm, and said in an excited tone, "You remember the guy I told you about, Alisha's boyfriend, remember?"

"The guy with the strange name: Mezz?" Sara said, thinking.

"Yes! That's him, that's the bastard," she said, pointing her finger at the Coffee shop that was located facing the lounge.

"Where?" Sara asked.

"Across the road," Trisha explained. "That guy in the coffee shop. Between those two guys', the one in white." She said, still pointing at them.

"Oh my god!" Sara exclaimed softly. "Why are you pointing at them; are you mad?" Sara jerked Trisha's hand away.

"Who cares!" Trisha said angrily. "He will get a slap from me if he comes to this side of the road."

"Who is the other guy?"

"I don't know him," Trisha replied. "Why, have you seen him somewhere?"

"No! He is cute." Sara said, taking another look at the boy who sat next to Mezz.

"Wait!" Trisha exclaimed, "Alisha must be upstairs, right? I am calling her right now. Just a second," Trisha said, taking her phone out and dialling a number.

"Oh god! you stupid girl." Sara grabbed Trisha's hand. "Let's go inside before they come here and slap us both."

They turned around and walked inside where their friends and the celebration waited. After the celebration, Trisha went home and Sara joined her lover, Nilay, in his car for a destination unknown to her at the moment.

"So, did you like the dress?" Nilay asked, talking about the birthday present he had given her, as he drove the car.

"It's amazing." Sara replied, her body turned towards him, her eyes focused on the road ahead.

"I knew you'd like it," he said. "When I saw this dress, I immediately knew that you're gonna like it. It's black and I thought: who doesn't like black; and also black looks great on you."

"Well, it's beautiful. Thank you so much," she said.

"And did I tell you that our band won as the best band at our college-fest?"

"Wow!" she exclaimed. "That's awesome," she said excitedly.

"Yeah, it was awesome. There were bands from all over India: Delhi, Bangalore, Mumbai, Pune, and some of them were pretty amazing. You should have been there. It was just mind-blowing; but we won because we had our own compositions that were beautiful. And our drummer was mind-blowing," he said, thrilled.

"And don't forget the guitarist," she said referring to him, in response to which he laughed proudly.

"I am just waiting for you to come to Mumbai," he continued. "It will be so much fun; I have also told dad to buy me a new car, so I am gonna throw my old car into the dump and buy this amazing new beauty."

"I am coming to Mumbai," Sara said, "as soon as my exams are over. My aunt stays there, so I am going to stay at her place, fill all my forms, and stay put."

"And once you get into my college, you and I will have real fun. I'll take a new apartment and we are gonna live together," he said comfortably. "You are going to love the parties. Just a few days ago, I was in this 36-hour party that had three different venues. After that I was so trashed that I slept for two days continuously." He laughed.

"When you told me you were sick?" She remarked.

"Yeah!" He laughed harder. "Sick!"

They both kept quiet. Sara was bewildered by the picture he had presented, and was dissecting it to find some possible good attached to it, while Nilay seemed lost in his memories, and was smiling and chuckling in a world of his own. Then he started to narrate many stories about himself and his friends, and in how many more creative ways they had wasted their money. And Sara seemed quite interested in listening to those anecdotes. They finally reached their destination–a tall apartment building. Nilay carefully parked the car.

In the elevator, she asked him, "Whose place is it?"

"It's mine," he said. "Dad bought it. The builder was a friend." He walked out of the elevator as the doors opened on the fourth floor, and Sara followed him. He took out his phone and checked the time, and said, "Perfect timing."

He opened the door of his apartment, and as it opened, Sara saw in the room, a bunch of Nilay's friends wearing colourful hats, all dressed up. One of them was holding a chocolate cake with a single burning candle fixed in the centre. All of them, after spotting Sara shouted, "Surprise!"

Nilay held her tightly in his arms, as she was in a state of shock and surprise, and very much taken aback by this unexpected gathering he had arranged for her. "Happy birthday, my love," he said, kissing her on the forehead while she wrapped her arms around him and held him as tightly as she could.

They slowly released themselves, smiling and looking into each other's eyes, and entered the house to join this party which was very different from the one they had recently attended. There was smoking, alcohol, loud music, and other friends. He gave a solo performance by playing songs he had written especially for her on his guitar, and after playing kissed her on the lips; and everyone roared and danced as the music roared with them.

After the party, she called up Trisha and told her that she was staying over at Nilay's place, and Trisha, without a question, vowed to protect her from her parents by making up a suitably good story. As the night approached, they couldn't resist staying distant from each other any longer, and started kissing as if they had been released after years of captivity. The transition from sofa to bed happened almost immediately. Nilay's hands moved all over her body: the places where she wanted to be touched and those that were strictly prohibited by her subconscious mind, which finally slapped her consciousness into awakening, and she pushed him away instantly.

"What?" he asked, breathing heavily. The buttons of his shirt had been torn or opened–she had no clue.

"I am sorry," she said trying to control herself. Nilay, on the other hand, after hearing those words whose meaning he understood as an invitation to resume the activity, moved towards her.

"Nilay, please! Just wait a second." Sara stopped him again.

"What happened?" He asked, confused.

"I can't," she said, "I am sorry." She started to look for her shoes.

"What?" Nilay said in confusion. "Are you leaving now? Can we just talk for a while?" His voice displayed that he had no clue how to react at the moment.

Sara sat down on the bed. "I am sorry," she said. "I am just acting stupid." She hugged him, tightly after saying those words. She wasn't wearing her coat anymore; her stockings were off; and some parts of her dress had clearly given up on protecting her skin from exposure.

"What is the problem?" He asked, taking a deep breath, and trying to think of talking rather than leering at her body.

"I can't do it, please!" she protested. "I don't want to take things too fast." She was standing almost at the edge of tears filled with responsibility and immense love for him.

"What?" Nilay asked in irritation. "Too fast? I thought we loved each other. I came from Mumbai to Delhi just for your birthday, for you." He rose angrily and walked away from her, waving his hands furiously. "If you were so unsure about me, you could have told me. I was f... dreaming about us living together." He shouted from the other room and came back.

"It's nothing like that," she said in tears. "I love you. Of course I do! I just need some time. And you came to Delhi for me, and you have me; why is sex so important?"

"What? You think I came for sex? I came here because I love you; and if I wanna just have sex, I can screw as many girls as I want in Mumbai. I don't have to come to Delhi to screw!" He said as he walked about in the room. "And the question is not about what I want, the question is: why can't we have sex? I am your boyfriend; you screwed your last boyfriend, didn't you? What is so wrong with me, or you loved him more than you love me? Are you still not over him?"

She looked at him with a blank expression; she had no idea from where to start, what to say, and how much to say, but she tried. "I love you more than anything, Nilay," she said in a firm voice, which was breaking from many parts. "I don't even think about him. What you just mentioned is the thing I regret the most now, and I don't want to rush anything with you. That's it!"

He immediately sat next to her and said: "but baby, we are never gonna separate." He kissed her on her left cheek. "Whatever we do together can never turn into something you'd regret. I won't let it become that, I promise you. You are my angel." And he kissed her lips again, and she kissed him back.

He gently laid her down on the bed, kissing her lips, and very smoothly unbuttoned his pants. He kissed her more, but she was still unwilling to submit to his wants, and thus kept a close check of where his hands were moving on her body. As his lips moved, caressing her neck and her arms, she found the self-control washing away from her mind, and felt more inclined towards dissolving into the arms of her lover. He slowly placed his right hand between her thighs and started fondling inside her dress which made her breathe harder. He interpreted that as a sign to do whatever he wished. He immediately pulled the strapless dress down from her chest, but as soon as he tried to fondle her breasts, she pushed him away –a lot harder this time.

"Stop!" She screamed, holding her dress.

But it was too late for the mildness in him to overcome the wildness that now overtook him. He leapt on her, grabbing hold of both her wrists in his fist, and placed them on top of her head. He forcibly lifted her dress up from her thighs, slid her underwear down past her knees, while she struggled hard to escape from the chains of his madness– and began to penetrate her.

Chapter - 6

Ayan scratched his chin, as he read once again from the top what he had written in the essay. He looked at his pen; at the decline of calligraphic grandeur in the long text he had written; and then looked around the room, filled with students doing exactly what he had been doing all this while: pouring out their thoughts the best way they could in their English Language exam. He looked at his answer sheet again, dismissing the element of momentary distraction lingering on his mind, and submerged himself into the realm of thought again. It was the last paragraph left to finish the essay, the last question of the board examination. And he began to finish his essay:

> As long as an evil person wears a mask of righteousness, he is considered not only acceptable as a social and cultural constituent of this society, but is esteemed and respected amidst the other mask-bearers, who form the governance and are responsible for the well-being of it-the basic foundation being that everyone wears a mask. But if ever an evil person decides to unmask himself verily guided by some sort of enlightenment or any righteous inclination, and decides to reveal his true nature to the world, with the prime intention of acquainting everyone with the truth; his existence, thereafter, becomes a mere blotch of infamy and extreme scorn. Such is the wisdom of society.

He sighed and looked at the bespectacled school teacher who was currently performing the role of a strict examiner. He had an unusually large nose and a big flat forehead like the blackboard in the same room, but in his case, the forehead wasn't black but tanned.

Ayan stood up from his seat and said, "Sir, I would like to submit my answer sheet."

The teacher walked up to him and took the sheet carefully. He rolled the answer sheet in his hands. "Okay everyone," he said loudly, "only five minutes left. Tie up your papers. I won't give you another minute after the time is up."

Ayan sat in his seat waiting for the minutes to be over, so he could leave the room. He thought about his essay, about the choice of topics that were mentioned in the question paper, and wondered: which topic would Mezz have chosen. He knew that Mezz would never choose a topic that would even mistakenly involve him to write what he felt personally, as he had a strict policy of mentioning only what the hearer wanted.

He took another look at the classroom, noticing the section of students buried in their answer sheets, employing their thoughts but mostly inclined towards reaching the word limit, which was, as taught to them by their teachers, most important. He noticed the other section of students, those who had also finished their papers and were sitting aimlessly like Ayan himself, playing with the pen by flipping it in the air or rotating it on the desk; or drawing figures on their question papers; or absorbed in thought looking outside the window. But Ayan wasn't bothered or influenced by the idleness provided in those five minutes, for he had an idea in his head, and therefore, stared at all those who sat around him, trying to relate his state to theirs, and putting himself in a self-recognized realm of superiority.

After the exam he stood outside the gate of his school, with an eye on the mass exodus of schoolchildren from the metal gates, waiting for Mezz to appear. He, unlike many of the students, found no connection with the giant school building when he saw it. All he noticed was a foundation of bricks, windows, doors, portico, columns and no life. He looked at the crowd again and spotted Mezz standing near the gate with three girls: all four of them deeply engrossed in discussing the question paper, which the girl in the shortest skirt was holding. Mezz noticed Ayan standing on the other side of the road, and therefore ended the conversation by saying something funny at which the girls laughed. He kissed their hands, and spoke a phrase in French. As the girls departed, smiling and turning back and smiling again, he walked towards Ayan, tearing up the question paper.

"So, how was your paper?" Ayan asked in a mocking tone.

"What?"

"That's what you were doing."

"That's what they think I was doing. And boy, I can do anything for them, those; whatever!" They both started walking casually down the same path they had chosen to walk everyday from their school to their houses.

"I have decided something," Ayan said. "I am going to start writing my first novel."

"Well, you know what? Even I have decided something. When do you plan to start?" Mezz asked.

"After the boards, of course!" Ayan said. "What's your plan?"

"I have decided to write a blog," Mezz expressed.

"A blog to teach all the loser guys how to court women properly. I have so much knowledge in this department."

"Let it do some good to the poor guy who actually needs it. And hell! I will earn some money out of it. I have been thinking about it from the point of view of going to college. I mean, some source of money would be nice."

Ayan carefully listened to him, and asked: "Law, right?"

"Yeah, man," Mezz responded. "Now I am positive. I need something that will give me a lot to read that I would love to read. Political science is a good option too." "Literature? Nah! I can read whatever I want to, it's all in the books; I don't need a degree for that. History: the same goes for it. And then there is what? Psychology?" He continued, "Psychology is tempting; it's my thing. But one has to compromise, and law seems more applicable and appealing to my nature and intellect," he said.

They both walked quietly for a while after which Ayan spoke, "Good for you."

"What is your story going to be about?" Mezz asked.

"Still forming it. Something related to history and love and fantasy and journey," Ayan replied.

"And war?" Mezz asked.

"Definitely war."

"It's not exactly the Indian taste," Mezz said, "If you know what I mean."

"Who is writing for a population?" Ayan replied. "A true writer or a philosopher writes for the one who will truly understand not only the meaning, but the heart of its creator; one who is destined to become the next great philosopher or writer of his own time."

"Damn right," Mezz agreed, nodding.

"So, which one are you choosing?" Ayan asked, referring to the three girls with whom Mezz had been discussing the question paper.

He looked at Ayan and smiled, "I don't know, man, I can't just do this to them. I can't be so inhuman, this low, this selfish. They are not objects I have the right to discard nor should I be treating them like sexual objects. They are beautiful human beings: each of them, special in her own way, with so much to offer and so much to hide; with so many secrets in their minds: all so naughty and mysterious and dark in their own ways; with so much to talk about their friends, family, future, fantasies, and everything that goes on in their delightful minds. Oh, what is there not to love in a woman; find me an answer and I shall never love again," he said poetically.

Ayan smiled and said: "So you are going to love all three of them."

"Yes," Mezz nodded. "You see, it's a curse. People think that I enjoy this but they can't possibly see the pain that I go through every day, after accepting this simple evident truth: that every girl in this world needs the beautiful, magical love I have to offer, which is the reason why they fall for me in the first place. Now, after realizing this fact, the most important thing is to control yourself with all the girls you date, but once in a while you meet a girl who changes and greatly affects this equation about self-control, and brings destruction to your peace. You know why?" he asked, looking at Ayan.

"Because she is a stalker, and she ruins your next relationships?" Ayan replied.

"Yes, that too!" Mezz said. "But the answer is: because she is a great girl, and you want to think about her. You want to know her in a better way, and talk to her all the time on the f…phone. You wanna go out with her, and see the world, and walk holding hands in the garden. And at such times, you feel like having her as your girlfriend, and getting serious. Taking all that magical love you have and showering it upon her to the fullest, forgetting all the girls you would have met and shared your love with in the future: being exceptionally selfish." He paused for a while.

"You think of loving this girl for your entire life, in each moment of your life, and even more if you can steal from death. Am I this selfish, my friend? No, I am not. I can't afford to know the fact that there are a thousand girls living right now in different parts of this world, who will be excluded from their right of experiencing this magical love, just because I committed myself to one. Oh, how disgusting is this thought! It's my destiny to meet every one of them and love them for a little part of their lives, regardless of having met the greatest girl of them all. I choose my duty to be supreme over self-satisfaction. And that is sacrifice, my friend. This is my curse." He sighed.

"No one knows the ugly side of the story except the

hero himself," he said.

They parted ways. Ayan walked along the road alone, and thought about the approaching deadline of the grand event that awaited him: the confrontation with Sara. He had carefully written her a new letter for that day, which explained his situation in the best possible way. It was the best of his letters. His house was not far away from Mezz's, and he could see the metallic gates of his house wide open and his uncle's car parked outside, which to him appeared slightly unusual in relation to the daily routine, according to which the car and his uncle were supposed to be at his office. His feet started to move faster, and his mind stopped working. He watched his uncle walking outside the gate with a strange worried expression on his face, which gave him the perception that something was not right. The moment his uncle saw Ayan, he called out, "he's here, he has come." He informed the other family members who were inside the house. "Come, Ayan," he said, and Ayan came running to him. His uncle's voice carried an unpleasant note that bothered him a lot.

"What happened, uncle?" Ayan asked in a worried tone.

His uncle had tears in his eyes which troubled Ayan even more. He hugged Ayan and broke down into tears like a child, which gave him an idea that whatever it was: it was more than terrible.

"What happened? Tell me," he pleaded.

"My son, there has been an accident, and we are going to the hospital right now. So get in the car." Ayan hopped inside the car without a second's delay.

"Whose accident?" he inquired. Ayan's mind was processing all the possibilities and names it could muster at the moment. "Who is it, uncle?" he asked.

His uncle signalled to the driver to drive faster. "It's your father," he said and started crying again.

Ayan was thrown into the greatest shock. He sat motionless holding his uncle in his arms. He checked the face of the driver in the rear-view mirror and found that his eyes were focused back on them but soon after noticing Ayan staring back at him, the driver looked straight ahead. His uncle was still weeping, but Ayan found himself helpless. What was expected of him, both in the eyes of his uncle and in his own, was to at least whimper, or break down, but all he could feel was nothing.

They reached the hospital in no time, and there he heard that his father had died of consuming excessive alcohol mixed with drugs, which resulted in his kidney failure: it was a compilation of the several theories and speculations that people discussed in tiny clusters in muted tones, whose bits fell into Ayan's ears as he moved from one spot to another. He saw his step-mother and her children all wrapped around each other, crying so loudly that they seemed to irritate the doctor and his staff; but they carried a perfectly adjusted expression which was situated somewhat between sorrowful and irritated. They were talking to his uncle about the transfer of the body from the hospital.

Ayan looked at them, took gradual steps backwards,

and walked out of the room. He found himself a spot to sit: a group of three metal chairs aligned outside every room, fixed to the ground. He relaxed there for a while, inviting thoughts in his mind, but none stayed in his head for longer than a minute, as his mind had been subjected to a state of chaos by the sight to which he had been exposed. And therefore, this moment of detachment from the scene inside the room gave him the opportunity to calm his mind, and as he began to think, the first thought that came into his mind was of Sara. He abruptly stopped himself as he believed that it was an insult to the memory of his father. But once again, she leapt into his mind, and he submitted himself as a faithful slave to her thoughts, and thought of his plans to meet her at the end of the board exams.

"Goodbye, Sara," he murmured which could possibly be the result of two inter-related reasons: first, the irritation caused by the inability to control his thoughts and keep her out; and second, punishing his heart for remaining so emotionless at the news of his father's demise.

The complete funeral proceedings took more days than his exams did, and no one–not even Mezz, bothered him for anything. He quietly gave his exams, and the school authorities helped the least by pretending to have helped the most. A month after the funeral, Ayan finally started to grow hair on his scalp, as going bald was one of the many rituals performed during a funeral in his religion. He was sitting with Mezz in his room, reading a book, while Mezz was engrossed in whatever he was watching on the television.

"Do you think I should have a girl as the protagonist of my novel?" Ayan asked.

"I think that is f... tough," Mezz said. "You have to put the woman's dramatis persona in your head and try to think from her point of view." He paused. "I am not saying that you can't do it; I am only saying it's too much unnecessary work."

Ayan smiled, "by the way," he asked, "how is Crash boomerang?"

"Who?" Mezz asked. "Oh, her case was over a long time ago. She had big time personality issues." He switched the television off. "Since you are talking about women – finally, I have to tell you something about Sara."

"What?" Ayan asked.

"She is in Mumbai," Mezz said, waiting for Ayan's reaction.

"In Mumbai doing what?" Ayan asked, wanting to know more.

"Applying to colleges, maybe," Mezz said. "All I know is that it has been around a month now, and also, maybe she is not coming back."

Ayan wanted to know the name of the source from whom he had gained this information, but remained quiet in spite of his doubts over the authenticity of the news. After a while, he forced his mind into believing that whatever he had heard was true. "So it's over," he said without any expression. "She is gone now, forever."

"Maybe, it is for good," Mezz added. After that, they

both talked about different subjects, their future plans, and Ayan's novel.

After having dinner with his uncle and family, he sat at his desk with a paper and a pen and wrote:

Dearest,

But before he could write anything more, he grabbed the paper crushing its perfect form and image in his hands, and broke down into tears, and cried unstoppably. He stood up after hours, his face wet with tears, and wrote:

5 May, 2005

What could be more upsetting than the simple truth that life is nothing more but the simple association of breath and emotions! You have to forgive me, my love, for not acting in accordance with the regulations of these requirements, which I have so blatantly ignored and extravagantly flouted. To what I have been subjected, I have no force upon, and yet as a slave I demand my rights. There is no true cause behind any victory because every cause plausible to a human mind is deluged with the paleness of thought, just like those of the shrewd mindless men of history, whose hopes of conquering have been proved worthless by time. For a very long time I have remained confused about the true meanings behind many concepts, and it is because of my interpretations and the attempts to continue thinking logically that I am in an enclosed room right now, with moist eyes, and completely unable to comprehend once again in my life: What is love and how is it greater than self-control?

Chapter - 7

Ayan was sitting in the centre of the mildly dark room, a fan over his head gloomily rotating at a speed carefully maintained not to blow the papers placed in several corners of the room, without any weight kept on them. On his right, there was a window with its white curtain that unconsciously barricaded the sunlight coming through, and on the left side of the window was a desk with papers and documents. On Ayan's left were two chairs similar in size and design to every other chair kept in that room. In front of him was positioned a table, and across the table, a chair. There were two portraits–one of a man and the other of a woman, that hung on two adjacent walls, and a round clock hung on the wall in front of him. It's ticking was the only audible sound in the room.

An old man entered the room and took the chair kept across the table facing Ayan. He was formally dressed in shirt and trousers, the colours of which didn't exactly complement each other, but he didn't seem to care. He kept quiet for sometime as he examined the list that he had brought with him, which had the names of the students he had to interview. He looked at Ayan and felt deeply insulted that the boy didn't care to speak a single word to acknowledge his presence, on the contrary, pretended to be completely ignorant of and unresponsive to the old man's presence. He picked up Ayan's documents and started to go through them rather casually until he noticed something, and said: "June 21st. It's your birthday today."

"Yes, sir." Ayan replied.

"Happy birthday."

"Thank you very much, sir." At this moment, two more gentlemen entered the room and placed themselves on the chairs that were kept on Ayan's left.

"So, tell me about yourself," the old man asked.

Listening to the old man's request, or formally his first question, Ayan seemed to be a little uncomfortable, and for the first time, his fixed body posture changed as he adjusted himself in the chair. This very question asked by the old man, according to Ayan required the wisest of minds to answer. But after observing the old man so far, he had understood that he demanded those nonsensical, fake answers that were prepared and made perfect in the mind by constant repetition; that were obvious and pleasant to hear; that had no answer in them but everything.

"My name is Ayan," he said in a different but confident tone. "And," he paused, thinking about what to say next, as he thought that everything was already given in his resume. He tried again: "Sir, this is one of the best colleges for studying English Literature, and," he stopped again.

"What happened?" The old man asked politely. "Don't be nervous? Just calm yourself down. Relax." He interrupted with the intention to help the boy.

"Well, sir," Ayan said, "to be honest, I am not sure about the conventional boundaries of such," Ayan paused for a moment trying to find the right word and said, "formal conversations."

The old man, a little surprised, replied, "That depends on what you have to say. Just feel free and leave it for me to decide. Okay?" Ayan nodded confidently. "So, shall we start again?" asked the old man.

"Yes, sir."

"Tell me about yourself now."

Ayan said, "Well, sir, I am a historical man. I dwell in the mysteries of Beowulf; I enjoy the sublimity in the words of Milton; I find grandness in the verses of Shakespeare; and seek knowledge in the endless writings of sages and philosophers."

The old man, a little confused over Ayan's answer, asked

him, "Why do you want to study Literature, and not History or Philosophy?"

"Look not into your past, but in your imagination, and you will find truths much greater than those you may learn from your mistakes," Ayan replied after a brief pause.

The old man smiled. "What do you want to do in your life?"

Ayan hesitated again but replied, "Sir, if a sentence could comprise the answer to this question, then the person is either joking about his life, or oblivious to the fact that he is alive."

The old man was slightly irritated with Ayan for not providing a straight answer but he remained calm and spoke again: "I meant, what do you want to accomplish in your life? What kind of job do you wish for?"

"I do not particularly relate myself to this man-made world," Ayan answered. "So these terms and designations do not fall into the dictionary of my perception. I have a completely different way of thinking over such matters, sir."

"Okay, I would like to hear what you think." The old man asked interestedly.

"As a learned human being," Ayan said, "the first objective is to truly understand what you know. And after you believe that you have understood the knowledge you have gained in your life, apply it to yourself and in your life, and observe psychologically as well as spiritually the fruits of it," he said slowly and clearly. "If it brings you satisfaction of a more peaceful kind and yields goodness as its result, then in this case your duty or job should be to make others understand this knowledge, those who are deprived of the capability to find it on their own." He paused for a moment.

"Apart from this," he continued, "in a very general sense which applies to everyone, the primary and most supreme obligation of every person is towards his family, society and self. If he is lacking in fulfillment of any of these three things, he can't be a part of any social association. If one is rude and uncaring towards one's parents, one is ungrateful, untrustworthy and an illiterate person of the worst kind. If one is lazy and non-performing as a citizen or a part of society, then it naturally becomes a diseased society. And one who does not think of inner satisfaction, I simply ask: who is he then?" And he paused for a brief moment.

"You see, sir, art is not for art's sake," he said. "And one who believes that it is for art's sake, the meaning of art for him, at one point, would become the disruption and perversion of truth. Art cannot be an end in itself, as imagination has no end; and without an imaginable end, artists have no purpose but to fulfill their own desires that are directed towards attaining beauty. And beauty serves the greatest joys in the greatest illusions." He paused.

"Are you saying that all the painters and sculptors and poets are misguided?" The old man asked, slightly challenged at this moment.

"No, sir," he said. "One who is stuck in the struggle to find beauty that is pleasant to the eyes, by looking into nature or at faces; through paintings or pictures, is enslaved by art and is not its" he paused thinking of the right word, "charioteer. What is art, sir? It's the purest depiction of the truth, and with the development of truth comes a moral duty: of spreading it. And therefore the law of control comes into motion. Anyone who treats any form of art as means to liberation from this world is not a societal being and is deeply selfish, despite the fact that he may produce the greatest of works from the perspective of beauty; but he would fail to produce truth and his works would live in dissension. Art, when working towards the end to produce truth, carefully supervised under the guidance of reason and logic and imagination, yields purity as its result. And it is only possible because it primarily requires control over one's mind."

"What is beauty then?" The old man asked, "Is it of no significance to you?"

"First of all, sir, beauty is imaginary," he said. "It is more truly felt than it can be seen, though there can't be much difference in the feeling one might get. Anyone enjoying a sight of nature, or viewing a beautiful painting is bound to be captivated, but one who enjoys the beauty that has no proof of its existence except only when it is felt, feels the true of nature of beauty. And there is nothing else in this world that can provide a purer evidence of the true nature of beauty other than music." He sighed.

"Beauty is in performance of the right action, and is the satisfaction one receives from it. It is in righteous thought. It is in true beliefs and an ideas. Beauty is in labour; it's in revolt. Beauty, sir, is in love." He paused, looking down and but not at anything.

"Accomplishments?" he said, thinking about the old man's previous question. "Accomplishments come into existence when you see life as a number. There is a form of intelligence beyond reason and logic, only understood by the enlightened: the universal truth." He looked into the eyes of the old man who was now quiet.

"What I do believe in is progress; which is transformation of a kind," he said.

"And transformation is not progress, but a process which, only in a few cases, yields progress." He paused. "Progress is divided into spans of time, which are fuelled by basic concepts, such as Inspiration, sir. And progress, generates both control and beauty. You see, neither beauty nor control can be achieved directly. They can't be an end to someone's work. You can't work towards bringing control in your mind, and nor can you achieve beauty by merely staring at oceans or over the mountains, as with time, you will tire yourself and give up, and if prolonged, your mind will demand something else and new."

He continued, "If a writer plans to write the best work of his life, then he will carefully choose what to write, therefore applying proper control over his mind; and at the end of each day, he will embrace the beauty of the product of his labor. You see, sir, beauty and control are the subconscious awakenings of your mind: when applied consciously towards a goal. Beauty and control are the by-products of labour towards a clearly defined goal. And happiness," he paused, "is the by-product of the two." Finally Ayan fell silent.

The old man took a deep breath. He smiled and said, "Okay, Mr Ayan, we'll sign out here."

"Thank you very much, sir," Ayan said, rising from the chair.

"So how old have you turned?" The old man asked.

"Eighteen, sir." Ayan replied and left.

At night while he was playing his violin, he constantly thought about the interview. He had another interview the next morning for the same course (English Literature) in another college that was equally eminent and prestigious. Those were the only two colleges he had applied to in Delhi.

After playing the violin he took out his notebook and pen, and started writing:

> Once upon a time there was a monster. He excelled in all kinds of warfare and destruction, and therefore took pride in calling himself the most powerful amongst his friends. As he grew up, his obsession with power and his monstrosity grew with him, and he wanted to rule the world. But then it wasn't easy as the people already had several kings divided according to lands, and one God they all worshipped. The monster didn't appreciate the order of things one bit, and killed a man. When he killed the first man, his family despised the monster. Then he killed a family,

and a whole clan of people despised him. Then he destroyed an entire clan, and the other clans around the destroyed clan feared him. Then he destroyed a city, and all the cities around the destroyed city feared him, and proclaimed him as their ruler.

But the monster was still not satisfied. He wished to be worshipped like God, as he believed he was no less powerful than him; in fact he believed that he was stronger than God. But when he asked all the people to worship him, they refused and he killed them all. He destroyed the entire cities which he ruled, and in rage, set out on a journey to find God, and to prove to everyone that he was stronger than God by killing him.

Years went by and he could not find God, but he didn't give up and travelled to places he had never thought existed. Wherever he went, he spread fear and killed many people in the pursuit of finding God, and finally one day, he heard about a man who knew where God was.

After finding him, the monster asked, "Do you know where God is?"

The man didn't flinch or budge. He replied, "Yes."

"Well, take me to him and I'll spare your life." The monster offered.

"Oh, well, you look like a generous being,"

the man replied. "Of course I will take you; but first, you'll have to tell me what business do you wish to discuss with him? What have you done so wonderful that I may take you to him?"

The monster got furious, but having no other choice told the man in great detail about the destruction he had caused; and then about his powers; and then about the fear he had spread amongst humans. The monster added: "I'll kill your God, and prove to the world that I am most powerful. And then, they will all worship me."

The man was very impressed, and said, "Whatever you have told me is certainly very hard to believe. I will take you to God under one condition, and that is if you take me to all the places you have destroyed, so I can see with my eyes and believe your words."

The monster agreed at once and they both walked in the direction from where the monster had started his journey. As they reached the place the monster once ruled, they both saw that it had changed completely. There were houses, markets, palaces, men, women, and kings.

"Where is the destruction? Show me." The man asked.

"It was right here. When I left years ago, there was not a single sign of life or buildings," the monster replied baffled by the sight.

The man smiled and replied, "Everything you destroyed has been re-created. There is no destruction now; no sign left of your work or powers. There is nothing like evil, but only a momentary illusion. What you are capable of destroying is lives and not life! And this is the power of God, not of destruction but of creation. Tell me, do you possess such a power?"

The monster kept quiet, unable to understand the situation.

"Then you are not more powerful than God," the man replied, and walked away.

The next day, he was sitting in front of four gentlemen–a partially bald man, who was smiling broadly while reviewing some papers and sipping tea from a cup with colourful designs on it; an old man with big glasses; a middle aged man with bushy eyebrows and a young man, probably in his thirties, typing something on his laptop.

It was a room similar to the previous one in which he was interviewed the day before, almost similar in the design and size of the chairs, the wooden doors, windows, desk, papers, the portraits and the clock. The bald man kept the papers down, and said, "Very good marks in your exams." Ayan said nothing, waiting to be asked a question.

"Tell me about yourself," he asked.

Ayan was not intrigued by the question due to its unintended repetition, and felt his stout honesty quickly evaporate. He told the man about himself, the name of his school, and the fact that he wanted to be a writer.

"That's very good. What kind of a writer?" He asked.

"A columnist for an International newspaper, sir."

The man smiled. "What are your interests?" he asked.

"Reading and Music," Ayan said softly.

"What is the name of your favorite book?"

Ayan thought for a while, trying to pick out the most obvious answer that retained its dignity. "*Plato's Dialogues*, sir." he said.

The man thought for a while as if recollecting something. "Tell me about Plato," he asked.

"Well, sir," Ayan said, "he was a student of Socrates, and one of the greatest Greek philosophers. His most famous dialogue is *The Republic*. He was also the teacher of Aristotle."

"And which is your favorite dialogue of them all?" The old man asked.

"*The Republic* only, sir" Ayan replied, whereas in truth his favourite dialogue was *Charmides*.

"And why do you like it?" he asked.

"Also tell us about the book," the middle aged man added.

"The republic is the very structure of Communism," he said. "It talks of an ideal state or Utopia, which is a state of a limited population, small in number, and the population is divided into three segments: the guardians, the soldiers, and the common people. Plato has greatly emphasized on education and Justice. Justice is in Book four, which basically tells us the importance of functional specialization and..." The bald man interrupted Ayan, asking, "Tell us your views on it?"

Ayan said: "Of course the idea of such a state is impractical, but there were two things that mainly intrigued me: first, Plato's teleological approach in everything he has written, keeping the end to be goodness; second, the exactness. Even though his state remained a dream, he pictured it to be alive and thought about the loopholes that would have been discovered by the corrupt, if it were in function; and he answered them. And that kind of smart thinking, sir, is impressive."

"Of course." The bald man agreed.

"You must have studied poetry. Which poet do you like the most in English Literature?" The old man asked. At this point, Ayan felt irritated by such questions; of course, he didn't have one name of a book or a writer in his mind.

"Shakespeare, sir. And Milton. And also Tennyson," he said.

"And how many plays of Shakespeare are there?" he asked.

"Thirty seven, sir."

"Are you sure that's the correct number?"

"It isn't," Ayan replied. "It is what the general consensus says."

"And how many have you read?" he asked.

"Only a few, sir." Ayan lied again, as he had read them all.

"And your favorite?"

"Troilus and Cressida, sir."

"You love history, don't you?" The young man asked,

speaking for the first time.

"What is there in history to love, sir?" Ayan replied rhetorically. "It's full of violence. But yes, I do love history."

The old man spoke again: "Have you ever been deeply touched by a poem; lines you could relate to, like your thoughts have taken the shape of words and have been presented to you?"

Ayan paused as he knew it was a smart question, a psychological question; and he thought of Ulysses, and then some of Shakespeare's sonnets, and finally spoke:

"Art is long, and time is fleeting. And our hearts though stout and brave,

Still, like muffled drums, are beating: Funeral marches to the grave.

In the world's broad field of battle, in the bivouac of life.

Be not like dumb, driven cattle! Be a hero in the strife!

Trust no future, however pleasant! Let the dead past bury its dead!

Act, act in the living Present! Heart within, and God overhead!" He paused, and looked at the old man. "These lines, sir," he said. "by Longfellow."

And that was the end of his interview.

After a few days the results of his interviews were out and, he found out that he had been rejected in the first and selected in the second.

Chapter - 8

"I am thinking about something," Mezz said, walking down to the market with Ayan.

"What?" Ayan asked. "What is the one thing that girls want the most from guys?" Mezz asked. "And which is the one way guys disappoint, or betray girls the most?"

"What and which?" Ayan asked, taking joy in his questions.

"Girls want friendship from guys," Mezz said, "Girls love to be friends with guys. I mean, they want to be friends with guys over girls. They despise their own sex." He paused and ridiculed: "How stupid is that, right? Anyway, the point is: Guys betray and disappoint them by falling for them after the friendship, basically by simply hitting on them. Always. And this is so overrated." He sighed.

"It's so expected from guys to react like that," he continued, "and I mean, regardless whether one successfully scores or not. It's not about scoring, but just the idea of wooing a girl in the same way over and over. It is as if there is only one door. I have introduced this new way: wooing a girl by telling her that you are gay. Can you picture it?" He asked, looking at Ayan, and chuckled.

Ayan laughed with him. "Actually I can," he said.

"By doing this, you indirectly assure a girl: that no matter what, the wooing is not going to happen; that you're not interested in her. And that is what women dig. Now who is going to try this new discovery of mine?" Mezz asked imperatively.

"Who?" Ayan asked.

"You."

"Yeah," Ayan said mockingly.

"You know what," Mezz said, "your wisdom is the enemy of your weenie; and one day your weenie is going to wage war against your wisdom. So it's better you start listening to me now." He looked at Ayan for an answer, but didn't receive any.

"No? Fine." He said. "You don't know about it right now, but you are going to woo a girl by being gay. How about we bet on it, a hundred bucks?"

"Yeah, hundred bucks, you are on," Ayan said looking at the other side of the busy road. They walked on without speaking for a while before Ayan asked, "How is your college?"

"It's okay," Mezz said, "Not so good for law. There are better colleges in other cities."

"Then why Delhi?" Ayan asked.

"Because I don't give a damn." Mezz said. "And I don't want to change that in myself. I mean, it doesn't bother me if I am not in such a good college, or I would get a shit job, or such stupid things. I am in the process of acquiring knowledge, not education. And who cares about a job? As if anything can stop me if I want one."

They reached the market and walked straight into a book store. While Mezz got engaged browsing through magazines, Ayan walked about the spacious store looking at the carefully placed books, notepads, mugs, cards, DVDs, and books. He picked up a notebook from a horizontal pile of notebooks kept on one of the many shelves, examined it carelessly, and suddenly felt a strong desire that he needed one of these. As he glanced back at the pile, he noticed a black-coloured shining notebook kept vertically in the left corner of the shelf with "A Thousand Letters" printed on its cover. He picked it up at once, and checked it thoroughly; it was meant for letters and contained more than a thousand sheets. He had not decided if he was going to continue writing letters to Sara; but at this moment, all such contradictory thoughts vanished, and he felt a strong relationship with the notebook as if both their destinies were intermingled.

"What have you got there?" Mezz asked Ayan as he spotted a giant black book in his hands.

"It's a notebook. See!" And he shared a glimpse of the black beauty with Mezz.

"A thousand letters," Mezz read the name. "Classy," he remarked.

They paid for the notebook and two magazines, and left the store. On their way back home, Mezz asked Ayan: "Have you started writing your novel?"

"Yeah, I have," Ayan answered nodding his head, "I am working on it now. Hey! why did you choose a hostel?" he suddenly asked.

"It's compulsory," Mezz replied. "I think for a year or two everyone has to. What about you? You could have stayed outside."

"I could but I have to work, you know." Ayan replied. "I only hope that I don't get some stupid pestering room-mates."

"Of course you are going to," Mezz confirmed.

"Well, thank you," Ayan said, and they both went to their respective houses.

After a few days, they both joined their colleges. Ayan had started working on his novel, and after he saw that he was sharing the room with two other students, he shifted his place of writing under a tree in the park near his college. He also used to take his violin with him but seldom played as the place was filled with anonymous students from other colleges who normally took a walk, sat in clusters and joked around as their laughter roared louder than thunder, clicked pictures from their cell-phones and ran up and down, and sometimes and in pairs of opposite sexes and disappeared behind the trees.

Ayan had recently been invited for the college fresher's party, to which he did not respond at all. But many a time he thought about going to the party, believing that he might gain an experience and find something useful for his novel. Finally when the day arrived, he was confused, which gave his room-mates ample opportunity to convince him to go with them to the party, and they all did.

After they came back to their hostel room from the party late at night, Ayan pulled his chair back from his study table in the dark room. Both of his room-mates retired to bed. He switched on the lamp, took a pen, and started writing in the new notebook he had bought.

> Dearest,
>
> I am perplexed, disgusted, and infuriated after looking at these over-exhibiting masks. What do they think? In such poorly improvised disguises, they raise their glasses in the pretence of having acquired dictatorial, demagogic powers. They are all artistic designs of an endangered species, and they are its own plague.

He rose from his chair, approached the only window in the room, and glanced out at the night. He looked at the sky but was unable to find the moon. His right hand reached into the pocket of his denim trousers, and he took out a packet of cigarettes. After having lit up a cigarette, he took a deep puff and exhaled the smoke into the darkness. "There you are; I can see you, air," he said, after which he came back to the chair and continued writing:

> Love,
> One who is not guided by any principles, a set rules of conduct for executing the most rudimentary plans in one's life: the very unimportant dealings that become of utmost importance if put together; that person will crumble without a sound and disappear into nothingness.
>
> As I have figured out today, the roots of the very concept of sins are trichotomous: sexual captivity (lust), ego (resulting in pride, competition, anger), and materialism (greed). Every other sin is an offspring of any one or a combination of these. And as we are so greatly influenced and ruled by these three satanic gifts, I wonder how psychology defines Goodness. I wonder how psychology defines a pure mind.
>
> The result achieved when one masters the mind by engaging extensively into the drudgery

of self questioning, self-analysis and the analysis of one's past?

Let's now discard the term 'satanic gifts' and contemplate the trio psychologically: the roots of evil (or sins) mentioned above are basically the very human instincts.

So, how can one ignore them and get rid of them?

They can't be finished, or easily ignored, but mastered by employing self-control in one's life.

How do we gain self-control?

It comes from the willingness to focus on a consciously and carefully chosen positive and spiritual motive. And since the roots of evil are instincts, self-control can't be developed by gaining knowledge from a source, introspection or retrospection. What comes out of these practices are conclusions, more knowledge if performed by a smart man, and regrets. Always remember: even the greatest of men this world has ever seen, were corrupt with competition, lust, pride, and personal ambitions.

And this simple fact divides humans into categories: those who never dare to look beyond their self are laymen; those who strive and struggle, and burn the midnight oil towards the betterment and change of self, those because of whom the world functions, are the smart men; and those who simply discard the existence of self are true great men.

No knowledge or above-mentioned efforts can transform or liberate a man from his instincts, except the experience of the very touch of one's end–death. Therefore, true great men are born, and nothing can thrust such divine greatness on any man nor can it be achieved by the same, as this very process is backed by certain degree of possibilities: circumstance, misery, and the sense of righteousness and wrongness. One makes a choice which makes that person outstanding, but the choice is offered to that person by time, and there is no true greatness in it. A true great man makes his choices long before time leaves his side, or misery forces him to break down, or circumstances wrong him.

So, what truly is greatness?

Greatness lies in a man believing in a righteous path so strongly that it conquers the fickle human mind to over-power or emerge regardless of any thought, actions or temptations that have the power to surprise, lure or influence him.

I don't maintain that every man who has been termed as great was a true great man, as people have never fully understood the meaning of greatness, and are too liberal with the labelling of it out of awe, gratitude, respect and envy. A great man is not one who can be proved great, but whose greatness can't be questioned, as proving requires argument, an argument requires questioning, and questioning directly points at the presence of flaws, loopholes or drawbacks.

Chapter - 9

Ayan always sat quietly in the class, and spoke only when he was asked to, or made part of a discussion. He noticed the girls who sat on his left engrossed in their cell phones, but never thought about them. He often looked outside the window, which was on his right but never bothered or wished to take a walk in the garden. He never looked straight ahead or read whatever was written on the blackboard, for two reasons: bad handwriting and good listening skills. Every day, he attended the class, sat idly, and as soon as it was over waited for another class, and if there wasn't any, quietly walked back to his hostel. In his room, he worked on his novel, read a lot, and did all the work that was assigned to the students in the classes. One day, after the class as he was walking back to his hostel he heard a female voice call his name. His mind was completely occupied with his novel's story, which is why he didn't pay any attention, but the moment he saw a girl walking next to him, he responded, "Yes?"

"Anna." The girl introduced herself. "Hi!"

"Hello," Ayan answered, "and what can I do for you?"

She was mildly surprised at his reaction and said: "Nothing. We are in the same class."

"Well," Ayan said, "it was very nice to meet you." And he started walking again, comparatively faster in order to ignore her. The girl, not getting offended, walked faster too.

"You're the quietest guy in the class," she said and waited for his reaction. None came. "And also the only guy who hasn't talked to any girl yet."

"Yet?" Ayan reacted.

"I don't know. You don't like girls?" She asked mischievously. He kept walking silently as he found the conversation purposeless, and concluded that the girl was a waste of his time. "You are also the smartest student in the class," she said, finally revealing the main reason for the sudden intrusion, "as quoted by Mr Murthy." The admiration did grab Ayan's attention and made him speak, "Mr who?" he asked.

"Mr Murthy! We just attended his class!" She said in a surprised tone, while he was still walking unaffectedly.

She continued, "he said that right after reviewing your assignment. He concluded that you are an exceptionally bright student. He didn't say that about anyone else in our class."

"And why did he tell you that?" Ayan asked, without any interest.

"Because I talk to him," she replied. "And I wasn't the only person there when he said that. He said that in front of many of our classmates. He is also helping us with the play..." Ayan interrupted her trying to end the conversation, "the play, yeah. I remember the announcement in the class."

"What announcement?" She asked in surprise. "There was no announcement." She looked at Ayan suspiciously and chuckled. "You have no clue about any play, right? I have never seen you texting on the cell phone. What do you do in the class?" Ayan didn't reply, and that offended her a bit.

They were walking along the concrete path that divided the garden of the college equally, leading one farther away from the building and closer to Ayan's hostel. Before he could tell her that his hostel was nearby, the girl, irritated by his discourteous behavior, reacted: "Listen, is there something wrong with you?" She asked, flaring up.

"Sorry?" Ayan said, completely taken aback.

"Tell me something, was I rude to you?" She asked in an angry yet reasonable tone. "Is it wrong to talk to a classmate?" She looked at Ayan, waiting for an answer, but he simply stood there, confused.

"Are you gay?" she continued. "If you think I was flirting with you all this while, because I came to know that you are really smart, then please! I talked to you because we are in the same class." She paused. "And I have a boyfriend."

Ayan felt partly guilty and partly confused over the sudden change in her behavior, and said: "Listen, eh…" He had forgotten her name. "Anna!" She helped.

"Yes, Anna," Ayan said. "I apologize for my bad behaviour. The truth is: I have been awfully busy working on something really important lately, and that is what was going on in my mind throughout our conversation.This sudden intrusion took me by surprise. I had no idea that I might hurt you. Please forgive me." Ayan spoke in a composed and calm manner.

"It's alright," she said and smiled.

"That's my hostel," Ayan said, pointing towards the building.

"I know," she said. They both shook hands, after which he turned around and walked straight without looking back. As he reached inside the hostel, he said to himself: "What the hell was that!"

Once inside the room, Ayan, sat on his chair, switched on his computer, and started typing his novel:

> The hands, exercising control over the typewriter, exhibited the picture of an entire machine and no human. The sight presented many ideas to understand what kind of a person he might be in

reality: the silent delusional writer, as his mind spoke of everything while he remained a tight-lipped iconoclast; or was he a loquacious breed of man, who in the absence of any company, conversed with his own mind, reaching into the depths of arguments. This night, he worked under the influence of a lamp, and was hypnotized by the breath of a broken heart.

Suddenly Ayan's cell phone started ringing, withdrawing him from writing. He picked it up, checked the screen, and found out it was Mezz's call. He answered, "Yep."

"What are you doing?"

"Nothing. Just back from College. Was writing the novel."

"Listen," Mezz said, "it's Sunday tomorrow. Come to my college right now; we will stay at a friend's place for the night, okay?"

Ayan paused for a while and replied, "Cool. I am on my way."

"Okay, see you. Bye." They both hung up. Ayan rubbed his eyes looking at the incomplete draft, and murmured, "by the breath of a broken heart? Terribly lame!" He saved it in his computer before turning it off. He looked at the clock but didn't think about the time. He lay down on the bed for a while and slept. Much later he heard his phone ringing.

"Where are you?" It was Mezz's voice at the other end.

"Oh, I slept. I am just leaving."

"What the hell! Come soon." And Mezz hung up.

All three of them sat on a wooden bench in a small park near Rishabh's house–where they had planned to stay the night. It was evening and the cool summer breeze with its utmost hospitality maintained the decorum of the surroundings, but the company of the bloodthirsty little flies sabotaged not only the convivial atmosphere but also any possibility of having peaceful thoughts.

Rishabh was tall and strong; tallest of the three, and stronger in appearance because lately he had been under a strict routine of working out and losing weight. The truth was: Rishabh used to be obese once, and he had suffered a depressing amount of rejections from girls on the grounds of appearance, and it affected him deeply, which was the reason why he had found in Mezz, his *Guru*.

Mezz had gained incredible attention in his college after courting a senior girl in the first month, a fact which irritated all of her ex-lovers, the hopeful candidates who had been lining up for years, the friends of those hopeful candidates, and those who have no business but to look for things to poke their noses into. All of these people decided to spread false stories about Mezz and the senior girl, to publicly shame and embarrass the girl, which would result in their break up–a plan that worked out very well, and did lead to their separation. But no one realized that, in all of this, they had given Mezz what he had primarily wanted: break up with the girl; and the entire college's focus on him. Out of this he got Rishabh as his protégé. He was extremely rich and he was not entirely dumb.

Ayan looked at Rishabh for a moment and was reminded of his incessant desire to smoke: a recent habit he had acquired from nowhere but to which he seemed to have clung quite dearly. While Ayan smoked his cigarette, Mezz turned to Rishabh and asked: "So Rishabh, do you believe in God?"

"Yeah," he answered, nodding his head.

"Which God?" asked Mezz.

"God is God."

"I meant which religion do you believe in?" Mezz asked.

"I am a Hindu, so Hinduism obviously." Rishabh replied.

"Then why did you say God is God. Do you know how many Gods are there in Hinduism?" Mezz said in a condescending tone. "Okay, which is your favourite God?"

"I don't have any favorite God or anything; I worship them all," Rishabh said in an uneasy tone.

"Oh come on, don't say that! There has to be one." "Rama, Ganesha, Hanuman, which one?"

Rishabh thought for a second, and repeated his previous answer in different words.

"Okay, tell me one thing: is this religion something you have consciously chosen over other religions after carefully studying all of them, or is it something you have inherited from your family, like everything else in your life?" Mezz asked, staring at him.

Rishabh, who was very sure where Mezz was going

with his question, took a defensive stand. "Dude, this is what I was born with," he said. "Everyone is like that. The things that you inherit become a part of your identity. It's natural. And it's really pathetic when some people, just to show off, try to follow or adopt stuff which they do not believe in just so they could be different or cool. People who change their identity are desperately craving for attention. All the f...ing hippies? What is that? The gothic culture? People who convert? They start worshipping and praying and following all that is given in the religion suddenly, like they didn't know about the existence of God before they had converted?" He stopped.

Ayan whose cigarette had almost burned itself out and reached its end, exclaimed: "Wow!" Mezz laughed, "So the bottom-line is: you have no clue about any religion and you have gladly accepted everything that was spoon-fed to you; along with it came religion too. If you were to be asked if God exists or not, you and I", he looked at Ayan, - "would hear statements such as: God is everywhere; look at nature, who can create it but God; if we have come from evolution, then why aren't the chimps evolving again?" Mezz spoke, changing tones which made Ayan laugh boisterously.

"Now maybe he'll start whining like a thirteen year old sissy girl," he paused, studying Rishabh's face. "Are you even a guy?"

"Yeah, whatever man," Rishabh said, in an irritated voice.

"Yeah, whatever man," Mezz said. "Hey cool it, Ayan.

Maybe it's the time of her month." Mezz, along with Ayan, laughed.

"You guys are assholes," Rishabh said, grinning as he looked at them. Mezz sat back and said: "I'll tell you what you believe in and what you don't. You are superstitious, aren't you?"

Rishabh admitted with a nod.

"You know why you believe in God?" Mezz asked rhetorically. "Because you were born with extreme fear in your heart."

"You are an insecure person who needs protection and guidance from something supernatural. You don't have the guts to believe in yourself, which is why every time you fail, you search for something to blame it on - time, planets, fate, whatever. And every time you find success, you give credit to the same elements–time, planets, fate, and bullshit."

"You need a moral code, because you are devoid of self-control, and therefore you need the fear of punishments for the so-called sins, which you so deliberately want to commit."

"You call yourself good," he continued, "and superior to the evil-doers around because you want to show that you are doing the right thing, but deep inside, you know what the truth is: it's not a choice you make to become a good man, you do it because you simply don't have the balls to be evil; and religion gives you plenty of scope to use it as an excuse to turn your cowardice into righteousness. You need forgiveness from God because there is no self in you, and if there is something, it is totally a stranger to you."

"You are not guided by your conscience," Mezz continued, "you can never think of reforming yourself from the mistakes you have committed, because all you seek is forgiveness from God. You need forgiveness from an external source because you have no self to rely on, and again, whatever there is, it is, from top to bottom, corrupt. You need God because you are a sinner, and the day you have to wash away the sins you have committed, you would want to be assured that there is a holy place to purge you; you want to keep in mind that there is salvation. You want to do good only because you want paradise after you die. You know what? You don't believe in God; you need God. You need God for yourself. You don't pray or worship just to be thankful." He paused. "And you know what that makes you? It makes you an asshole, get it? You're an asshole." He looked at Ayan and asked: "What's that quote by Voltaire?"

Ayan responded: "If God did not exist, it would be necessary to invent him." Mezz winked at Rishabh.

All three of them stayed quiet for a minute, after which Mezz turned to Rishabh, smiling. "What?" he asked.

"Nothing, dude," Rishabh replied in an irritated voice. "If you are an atheist, what can anyone say?"

"What?" Mezz cried, "Who gave you this idea! I believe in God. But allow me to present you with a perspective. There was once a thinker who wrote: If oxen and horses and lions had hands and were able to draw with their hands and do the same things as men, horses would draw the shape of gods to look like horses and oxen would draw them to look like oxen, and each would make the god's bodies have the same shape as they themselves had. Now obviously he was talking about the Greek anthropomorphic gods, but this applies to religions alive even today. After all, God made humans in his image. Now isn't that a tiny bit suspicious? I mean, God created the whole universe, why does he have to come down to earth of all the planets in the infinite universe–which if you study you'd find is pretty big–and start becoming a part of every person's life? But forget it, dude, you won't get it anyway."

Chapter - 10

4 September, 2005

Dear Angel,

I thought about beauty today, and in some way, entirely subconsciously a poem with the title 'the silent armor' came into my mind. I am pondering about this strange analogy, and simultaneously, I have reached the extent of thoughts regarding beauty. One part of my mind is consumed by nothingness, captivated entirely by the magnificence of the image of the supernatural non-understandable agent that exhibits beauty -

which is basically the common reaction of every human. The other part of my brain is silently sad about the fact that beauty fades away with time, and if I capture it at this moment, by taking a picture or drawing it in its perfect image, I am clinging onto a past that is yet to come. Another part of my brain is pondering about the tragedy of beauty, and all its admirers who submerge themselves into it. How sad it is, that a thing of beauty is not a joy forever, and as the greatest teachers have told me along with my rational mind that beauty is to be ignored and perfection to be tasted only, and then forgotten, and then tried again. But then why are we slaves to beauty, and slaves to the forms of art that require and rotate around the axis of beauty only?

I want to erase the part in which I adore your beauty, fanatically involving myself like a murderer of every thought that is gasping for survival, for love has taken over in my mind entirely. Yesterday, I saw a dream, a dream which occurred when evening looks like morning, where I can't decide what is more beautiful: sunset or sunrise. I was fully occupied in a beauty that my naked eyes could perhaps recognize, until I saw you. Beauty has its own spell, and the one captivated by it is either a fool or a slave; one in love with it is either an artist or a philosopher; and one who possesses beauty is an angel in suffering.

Ayan stopped writing, closed the notebook, and looked in front of him at the people who were in the park. He had been sitting under a tree, a fixed spot within a triangle formed by three trees, and he always stayed inside the triangle. He had written several more letters to Sara, but the number of letters per month kept declining as time progressed. The truth is: he was too busy attending classes, reading in the library, and also writing his novel, the time for which he had to steal. But he was satisfied with his work in the book.

His eyes fell on a girl sitting on a bench, which was located just next to the cemented pavement in the park, and he immediately recognized her–it was Anna. He wondered what she was doing there, sitting alone; and thought of two and three possibilities, and for the first time, he examined her as a girl. She was tall, slim with straight black hair, wore everything black that complemented her white skin and brightened her deep red lips. She had big black eyes that changed shape with her expressions and words; she had a beautifully carved nose that reminded Ayan of a peacock. She wore expensive clothes and never repeated them, which indirectly asserted that she was affluent. He also thought she was different as he had not seen her meandering around with a group of girls. She never carried bags similar to other girls but carried a backpack. He stood up with the intention of walking back to his hostel, picked up the violin's case and his notebook, and started walking towards the bench. "Hey," he said, standing behind the girl.

"Hello!" Anna said, turning around and spotting Ayan standing there, wearing a black polo cap, a plain Tee and denim trousers.

"Waiting for someone?" Ayan asked.

"No, just sitting here alone," Anna replied. "Wanna join?"

Ayan looked around, took a deep breath, and asked, "What's bothering you? You look stressed."

"I am never stressed." She looked straight after saying that, smiled, and looked back at Ayan.

"How are your studies going?" Ayan asked.

"You know what, that's why I am stressed," she replied.

Ayan put his violin case on the ground next to the bench and sat there. "Tell you what;" he said, "let's play a game. It's called free therapy session. Tell me whatever you think are the causes that keep you away from books, anything from your friends to typical mood swings, anything; and I'll tell you what your problem is. But remember, what I'll tell you won't be suggestions or what I think. Treat them as facts, because that is what they are going to be."

She was a little surprised at his sudden interest and felt mildly confused for a second, but after she weighed his last words she was forced to drop her doubts and start the simple sharing of thoughts "Well," Anna said thinking, "laziness?"

"Keep going," Ayan said, "Just feel free and think of everything that might be a reason."

"I don't know!" she said. "It's the huge amount of work. And lately I have been hating going to classes too. I am also losing interest in Literature; maybe it is the thing that we are studying right now, but I don't know." She stopped.

Ayan immediately spoke: "There could be many reasons behind these reactions and such behavior.

Let's suppose it is all chronological, and it started from laziness, and laziness resulted in the accumulation of all the work that you have been ignoring into huge piles; thus resulting in the huge amount of work. Now because of this pending work, you started to find the classes boring, and repelling due to more writing, reading, and all sorts of work that is assigned in them. And finally all of it resulted in your neutrality towards Literature, or" he paused, "You have made the wrong choice and mustn't be studying Literature in the first place. So, which one is it?" he asked.

"No, I love literature," she said with confidence in her voice. "It's not the wrong choice, it's just lately that I have," she paused... "I don't know."

"So, it's your boyfriend." Ayan asked.

"What?" she said in a surprised tone. Ayan sensed that he had said something he shouldn't have.

"If you love something" he said, "you can't be distracted from it this easily. Obviously one gets distracted because of an external stimulus that is superior and more important, which in your case would be selfish love."

"Do I look this predictable to you?" she defended aggressively.

"Am I wrong?" he asked frankly.

"It's none of your business," she said, putting an end to the conversation.

Ayan sighed. "But a little insight won't be too harsh, I guess," he said. "You see, people like you have the tendency to engage themselves in certain very usual activities that involve maximum time consumption, so at the end of the day, they are naturally unable to work. And out of such activities there are a few activities that have the property of transforming themselves into something that can be called as work, which make people like you, believe that they have worked, and provide themselves with partial satisfaction." He paused.

"You get irritated easily, because you are unable to refute the biggest confrontation, which is time; and because of that you invite stress. You search for entertainment through stupid means. You become impulsive and irrational, and blinded towards the real problem, and focus only on trivial problems. And after people like you solve those trivial problems, they do gain satisfaction; but in most cases, they forget what their real problem is, and invite frustration and mood swings as permanent features in their behavioral structure, until the real problem is resolved."

He continued, "then some people, subconsciously look for distractions and invite unwanted human association in their lives which is more likely to waste a lot more of their time thinking about something that is not even related to their lives." Ayan stopped, gently picking up his violin and the notepad, and spoke for the last time in this conversation: "Perhaps, this is enough for you. Remember the facts. And lastly, I am sorry to have mentioned your boyfriend." He stood up and left, leaving the girl silenced.

At night, he received a message from Anna on his phone:

> Hey, I am really sorry about today. I have been thinking about what you said all day. Can we please forget what happened and be friends again? Please please please?
>
> Love
> Anna

The first thing that crossed Ayan's mind was, how did she manage to get his number; but then, after calculated thinking he narrowed down many possible sources. The second thing that he thought was: whether he should message her back or not, which he did, with great difficulty.

It's ok. Everything is cool.

After this meltdown, they both met and talked quite often–in the park, or after the class–but didn't decide to take it any further by planning to meet. The truth was that he was so busy and fascinated by his novel that all he did was think about the story. He didn't care much about Anna and thought of her only as an acquaintance, which was the reason why he didn't mention his novel to her, although she often wondered what kept him so busy and occupied.

On a Sunday evening, while Ayan was returning from the park, he was rudely stopped by three boys. The one who started the dialogue was the youngest of the three: "You're the one who loves to be a womanizer right?"

Ayan was surprised. He maintained a straight face, and

made no attempt to show that he was confused.

"I think you've got the wrong guy."

"No, we have got the right guy," the tallest boy said, emphasizing on the 'we'.

"Then I don't follow you," Ayan said. "Maybe you have misunderstood something that I can help you with, by providing facts. Shall we come to the point?"

The youngest boy shouted, "I am talking about Anna, you asshole." He was interrupted by the third boy, who hadn't spoken anything all this while, and who finally did speak: "Do you know who I am? You think you are tough with that attitude, you smartass motherfucker! You'll be buried here if you even say another word." He moved closer to Ayan. "You understand?" he asked, knocking on Ayan's chest with his index finger.

Ayan said calmly "I have never been in a fight, it's true; and there is no way I would be able to do anything if you all started to beat me right now. But there is one thing that I used to do a lot when I was a kid: I used to bite whenever I was angry." He smirked. "And you know who I bit the last time in my life; it was my dog." He looked at the tallest boy. "It was the dog that bit me first, and that hurt, so I bit him back and he died. But here's the secret, I didn't bite my dog as a counter-attack, what my mother and everyone thought, I bit because his bite hurt me. I was angry."

And he looked at everyone. "But I am sure you'll only punch me, and I know for a fact that it won't hurt me as much as a bite would, but I hope it does. I really hope it does." And he smiled wickedly. "I could never find out if I can ever do that again," he said to himself, "until now. Finally!" Ayan looked at the three boys who just stood staring at him; he turned around and walked away.

After he reached his hostel, he took his cell-phone out and called Mezz.

"Hey," Mezz responded.

"Yeah, listen," Ayan said, "I have got a problem, but it's a chick problem. Where are you?"

"What happened?" Mezz asked.

"There were some guys here, bullshitting me with their crap."

"Oh, wait then, I am on my way." Mezz hung up.

He reached Ayan's hostel with Rishabh within half an hour, and it took Ayan another fifteen minutes to narrate the entire scene. After listening to it, Mezz replied: "Listen bro, the only reason a guy comes running with a baseball bat, or with a bunch of his daddy's hired goons is when his girlfriend has been blabbering about you. There are three situations in which it becomes crystal clear to the guy that his girlfriend is going crazy: first, if she repeats your name more than thrice in a single conversation; second, if she talks about you for more than fifteen minutes in a conversation; and third, if she starts comparing her boyfriend with you. Whenever any one of these three things is blown out of proportion by a chick, the boyfriend goes running to the guy. But my point is: it's not the guy, it's the girl."

"We are not even friends," Ayan protested.

"Anyway, what's the name of the guy?"

"Don't have a clue," Ayan said, looking outside the window

at the sky.

Mezz scratched his head and took his phone out, "Well, we do know the chick's name. I'll get her boyfriend's name out." He signalled to Rishabh and told him to call a certain someone.

"So, you like this chick?" He turned around to Ayan and asked.

"No," Ayan said, "Nothing like that. She's in my class; I can't avoid her."

"Don't worry, I will get every detail about her." Mezz said with a little mischief in his voice, while Ayan took out a cigarette and started smoking.

"It's about the drama," Ayan said, "I don't want all this shit outside the college. And she is smart; we have never had anything going between us. You think I should talk to her about this?" he asked Mezz.

"Are you f...king kidding me?" Mezz reacted. "She wouldn't know anything about this. You're not thinking, Ayan. Think: Why would her guy come to stop you if he can stop her? Obviously their relationship is messed up. Let me tell you one thing very straight: this chick is falling for you, and I don't know how much you guys talk, but understand the truth before it becomes reality," he said.

"Well, I don't think so," Ayan said thoughtfully.

"Whatever suits you, my man," Mezz said, "The thing is, you won't be bothered by anyone from now on."

Chapter - 11

As he pulled his shirt off, a weak body appeared, weakened from every corner of the muscles it held. He saw himself in the mirror with a severe ache in his head and he saw his feeble eyes, as if immense pain had caused them to erode. He stood up in moral disgrace as every breath of his demanded acquisition of wellness, and he sat down with a peculiar but common physical disgrace.

Ayan stopped and took a conscious breath. He was very close to the end of his novel, and during this period, his devotion towards the book had increased more than anything else in his life. He had been writing for ten to twelve hours every day; he would have written more if he didn't have classes to attend. He stopped because his phone started ringing. "Hello!"

"Hey, what are you doing?" It was Mezz's voice. "I am getting bored. I am coming to your college, if you are not too busy with your book."

"No, not at all." Ayan answered.

"Okay, I will be there in an hour or so." And he hung up.

Ayan stretched and placed his hands on the keyboard of his computer again. Before he could type anything, another different ring emanated from his phone, but the sound wasn't the one of a call, it was of a message. He picked up his phone and read the message. It was Anna's:

Where are you?

Ayan replied:

Hostel.

Anna's reply came after a few seconds:

Meet me in the park.

After the encounter Ayan had with Anna's boyfriend, it was obvious that their next meeting would certainly bring up the subject, but when they met, Ayan found that she was clueless about it. He even thought about narrating the entire incident to her but after he remembered the dialogues exchanged between him and the boys, especially his part about biting the dog, he preferred silence.

"Hey!" He said softly.

"Hi!" Anna said with a sad and troubled expression.

"What's the matter?" Ayan inquired casually sitting next to her on the bench.

She replied nothing, which was a sign that she had much to say, but such a casual concern was too much of an insult for her to give in to. Ayan remained quiet and looked across at the people who were in the park; his eyes noticing a group of young people, probably of some other college, laughing loudly amongst themselves attracting everyone's attention.

They both sat quietly for a minute before Anna spoke, "I wanna discuss something with you, since you can understand things."

"What is it?" Ayan asked.

"It's about my relationship," she replied.

Ayan, a little alarmed by those words, forgot the young people and turned to her. "What do you want to discuss?" He asked.

"I am not sure about anything in my life right now," she said. "And it's affecting my studies, like you mentioned that day, and I don't want that to happen. My grades haven't been satisfactory and I couldn't even respond to my father when he asked what I had been up to!"

"You're telling me the outlines. Get into the real stuff," he said.

"I used to love my boyfriend, and I still do," Anna said. "But lately, I have started to avoid him and stopped taking his calls, and that really pisses him off. But what he doesn't understand is that I need some time. Whenever I am talking to him he asks me such stupid questions, or accuses me of being disloyal and dishonest to him, just because I can't answer him. He doesn't understand that I am confused myself, and I only need some time."

"Time for what?" Ayan asked.

"Time to clear things for myself," Anna answered.

"And what if you are wrong or unable to?" Ayan asked.

"Then I have no clue," she answered. "Maybe I should just die." And she buried her head in her hands.

Ayan smiled and asked, "What about your friends?"

"They are supportive," she said, "but I don't need their support, or sympathy, or just a listener. What I need is a solution."

"Confirmation," Ayan corrected. "You need confirmation and that is why you are not open to anything else." He paused, waiting for her to raise her head. "Do you love him?"

"Of course I do," she said confidently.

"Why do you love him?" Ayan asked.

"What?" She replied in a confused manner.

"Things that make you love him, just think, and remember, and tell me."

"He is a nice guy. He is like a cartoon: always making me laugh, cracking jokes, doing all kinds of pranks." And she smiled, remembering, "He never dominates me. Actually, I am the one who is dominating in the relationship." Ayan kept quiet, listening.

"And for how many years have you been together?" Ayan asked.

"Four."

"How is he as a companion?"

"He is a nice guy and he really loves me. What do you wanna hear?"

"Define him in one word."

"Well, I would say: extremely adorable. Cute. Yes, cute," Anna replied. And Ayan stopped his questions and looked straight ahead again.

"Okay, say it now," she demanded.

"Look, your relationship and the love that you share with him, they are both spotless. But your problem is an eventuality that not only connects with you, but connects with the very nature and requisite of any woman," he paused. "understood anything?"

"Except for blah blah blah, nothing," she mocked.

"Okay," Ayan said, "picture your boyfriend in front of you now, and think of everything that you mentioned a while ago. What is he to you? He is childish, immature, caring, loveable, honest, adorable, very cartoon-like."

Anna interrupted, "I was only giving you an example by saying the cartoon type..." Ayan resumed, "Shut up and listen to me. Forget what you said. I am talking about the definition of an ideal man, and he stands nowhere even close to it. Your affair with him blossomed and nurtured at the time when you were a kid. And of course all the things that you have mentioned about him would gladly charm a fifteen-year-old, but at this age, when you are no more a juvenile the same actions that once entertained you are the ones you have a problem with." He paused.

"And because of the absence of such a figure in your life," he continued, "except your father, who I believe is rather strict and terse, I shall conclude that you will not appreciate a personality as your lover to guide you. You would rebel agaisnt at such a thought, wouldn't you?" Anna was quiet and sat immovable as a rock, a reaction that confused Ayan.

"Nevertheless," he continued, "this is the reason why you have continued your relationship with him for so long, because he allowed this part of you to stay and grow. It has never been challenged or tested. But now the real question is: do you really want to be guided?" Ayan asked softly.

"No. Why would I want that? I have always made my own decisions, and it is not that he is completely dumb or anything. He is smart. And I find it to be a good thing that he is not the guiding types; I do not like a man to be guiding me. I can take care of myself."

"Really?" Ayan asked. "Do you want an example of a man guiding you?"

Anna said yes with her eyes.

"It's happening right now," he said.

"Fine, I am leaving," she said, standing up.

"No no no, don't be that defensive! Sit down." Ayan pressed her hand and made her sit. "I just want you to know that it's not something wrong. And it's certainly not a sign of weakness. We are just having a conversation, aren't we? And of course you don't want to be guided, but the complete sentence is: you don't want to be guided by him. The day you'll meet a man whose intellect, reason, and logic will be unquestionably superior to yours, you will not subdue his words; or would you? Because if you would, then you are nothing but a self-obsessed, narcissistic being, and I am wasting my time. But because you are not, you will invite the reason of that man to enter your mind. I think you have confused the idea of seeking guidance with being controlled; and secondly, it's the very nature of your boyfriend that has added such strong characteristic beliefs in you. It's not a day's work; it's what you have become by constant repetitive exposure to his personality to which you have adjusted only because of love," he said and waited for a reaction.

"What should I do then?" She asked, giving up.

"Look, it's about your love," he said. "And I don't know anything about it; how can I even say it is true love, or that you'd be incomplete without him. Just answer me one thing, and in that answer you will have your answer, okay?"

"What?" she asked attentively.

"Suppose you sort out everything with him, even if you have to apologize. Please close your eyes and picture in your mind: that you go and have a talk with him, and everything is resolved. You are giving your relationship another chance by bringing it to that very level where it is happy and okay. Think that you have started anew and for once everything is back to normal. Now, ask yourself this simple question: Does this scenario feel, anywhere in your mind, like a compromise?"

Anna was quieter than quiet at that moment. Ayan took

his cell phone out. It had been vibrating for quite a while in his pocket. He called a number. "Hey, where have you reached?" he asked.

"On my way. Where are you? Why haven't you been picking up?" Mezz answered at the other end.

"Well, have you seen that park, the one close to my college?"

"The park in which you write?" Mezz asked.

"Yeah, that one. I am there," Ayan answered.

"With a chick?" Mezz asked.

"No," Ayan said, "I am alone."

"You're kidding me now? The black denims, grey pull-over, fair chubby cheeks?"

Ayan smiled. "Why can't I see you? Which tree are you hiding behind?"

"I am on the road. Don't let the chick go." Mezz said and hung up.

Ayan turned to Anna, "Listen, a very good friend of mine is coming. There he is," he said, pointing at Mezz who was now visible entering through the tiny metallic gate of the park.

"Oh, I'll leave then," she said, standing up. "No, don't leave, stay. You need company right now," Ayan said, standing up with her.

"Hey!" Ayan said to Mezz. They gave each other a hug.

"This is Anna. Anna, this is Mezz." Ayan introduced them.

"Mezz? What's your real name?" Anna asked, smiling.

"So, you are the Anna? Wow! It's a pleasure to meet you, not pleasure, actually it's a blessing. And to be honest, you are a million times more beautiful than the picture in my mind, which he painted using his words." Mezz pointed at Ayan, and then looked into her eyes smiling while Anna blushed. "Come on," Mezz said, "let's all take a walk." And they started to walk along the cemented pavement.

"What do you do?" Anna asked Mezz, and he told her the name of his college and about the course.

"Must be fascinating, studying Law, isn't it?" she asked.

"Not as fascinating as taking a stroll with a great thinker and such a beauty," Mezz answered and Anna blushed. "What do you think about love, Anna?" he asked swiftly.

"Well, right now, I have no idea." She giggled.

"In fact we were just discussing love," Ayan said. "Come on Mezz, enlighten this girl now. Make her illusions go away."

Mezz smirked, "Love is the degree of amusement between two individuals, and the longer the amusement stays, the couple remains intact; but the moment the amusement dies or fades away, both the individuals, subconsciously, start to look for other partners as a means to ignite the amusement they once shared and individually demand." He looked at Anna for her reaction.

"This is the reason why most break-ups occur; the same reason why guys wonder," he spoke in a deep voice to imitate a grown man, "why the hell did she pick this guy over me, especially when I am better-looking than him? The same reason why women get attracted towards artists, or musicians, or guys with a good sense of humor. It's all a part of entertainment. Look at marriage counselling; I mean, come on, all the articles and books on how to spice up your marriage? What is the word they are talking about now?" He paused. "Amusement. Why do you think womanizers are such a big success? There are many reasons, but a very important one is simply because I never date a girl long enough for the amusement between us to die." He paused.

"But," he said, "there is a trump card to amusement. Love is the degree of amusement between two people, unless there is a bigger selfish motive involved; for example: the guy is a multi-millionaire. Then, it's the degree of amusement plus a future, and so the degree of amusement gets superseded. The reason can be any; the stable future was only an example."

He said thoughtfully, "This concept proves that a human mind works in accordance with the subconscious wants of people, which they have no clue about; and not their conscious, theoretical wants–which they believe they actually want. And it is these stupid wants that give birth to notions such as true love. So, now you can understand how non-existent true love is." And he smiled, looking up at the sky as if being embraced by God for spreading absolute knowledge. Ayan smiled while Anna was still lost in his words, all three of them walking on quietly.

After Anna left, Ayan talked to Mezz privately. "You were right that day," he said. "She has found in me her ideal man, because of which she is having problems with her boyfriend. But she hasn't understood it, though I think I might have helped her today. I am pretty sure she'll realize it soon."

"I am happy for you," Mezz said.

"What are you talking about?" Ayan asked. "Help me here."

"Then stop talking to her," Mezz suggested.

"It isn't that simple anymore," Ayan said. "She reached out to me for help today. It means something to me as a human being."

"Then tell her about Sara before she confesses."

"Are you kidding me?"

"Well, in that case, there is only one option. Tell her that you are gay," Mezz suggested.

Ayan looked at Mezz in wonder, "You asshole," he said, "for hundred bucks?"

Mezz laughed, "I knew you would say that, but listen to me: it's not about you; think about that poor guy who could really be in love with this girl. Forget about what he tried to pull off that day with you! But think, if she decides to break up with that guy, backed up by your thoughts, or dreams that your presence has provided, she will not think or consult you before doing it. All she is going to do is come to you, smile in happiness and say: I broke up with my boyfriend. And then you will feel the sting. And, with that will come the guilt. But you know, what's the worst that will come?" He softly whispered two words into Ayan's ears. "Her responsibility." And those very words sent shivers down Ayan's spine.

"Do you remember what I said when I was talking about the method of wooing a girl by being gay?" Mezz asked rhetorically. "To complete this method, to finally woo the girl, one has to confess that one is not gay by giving reasons such as: I wasn't ready for emotional attachment, or didn't want a relationship. But who is asking you to do that? Tell her that you are gay, be friends with her, and this way she knows there is no future with you, and she sticks with her boyfriend. And you won't fall for her because you are already in love. And because you guys won't be together, I will not win the bet; how about that now?"

Ayan took a deep breath and said, "I'll think about it." That night Ayan messaged her:

I want to tell you something, I am not straight. Not everyone knows except a few people.

I hope you can keep this secret.

He waited for her reply but it didn't come, and so he busied himself in sending e-mails to many publishers in India about his novel.

Chapter - 12

16 May, 2006

It's extensively remarkable, to observe her in this present state of her life which when compared to her former state, yields an outstanding reformation. It is not very surprising that I am being suspicious of her strange, although truthful and unintended actions that raise doubts and questions. I prefer to think now, of such actions in a man, as a constant yearning for acquiring the desired objective, and as there is never an end to desires, the continuance of such a chain of events has no end. I shall not take it as a defeat of some sort even when I hear in her voice a slight whisper of lies and infidelity towards her chosen principles. But rather I should focus on the attempts to help her towards betterment, with the hope to retrieve a balance between the very nature I detest and the hero that is inside her.

I believe what she is striving for, is what she wants to do, and would continue to perform in the future, whereas my focus and quest deals with her evolution and not with her corporeal demands, or acquaintances, or the story of her life.

She is a layman, and that she will always be.

Ayan stopped typing and saved the draft. He used to write about Anna often, keeping a record of her behavioral performances that seemed to rise and drop like lines on a graph. The truth was that after the completion of his novel, his concern had shifted greatly to Anna's life, and after securing himself by expressing his false sexual orientation, he was free to befriend her. As a result, they had become very close friends. The truth was that like Mezz, Ayan had, for the first time, chosen a protégé too– Anna. But there was a vast difference between their methods, teachings, dedication, and sanctity. Both Anna and Ayan were oblivious of this little arrangement between them, and they walked regularly in the park. Ayan talked about the connection of man with the universe, with God, with

Nature, with society, and with himself. He taught her how to read a person by observing his personality, his words, and find out what was going on in his mind. And then they talked about chaos, panic, satire, and manners. He talked about God, concept of religion, ancient civilizations, and the history of religious sacrifices. And then he talked about great books and men such as Homer, Pythagoras, Valmiki, and Vyasa.

These regular walks continued for months, uninterrupted and uninfluenced by any force or unfortunate event crossing their lives. In those one or two hours, they would expel themselves from the realms of their bodies and were exposed to something strange where emotions for one another died; but they were alive again, when they lived their normal lives without each other's company–that is when they thought of each other and emotions started to build, less in Ayan's mind and more in Anna's.

It had been a year now since their colleges began, and Ayan decided to leave the hostel for good. In a three hour chat with his uncle he was told that his father had left him an apartment not very far from his college. His uncle's original plan was to tell Ayan about the apartment after he had finished his course. But because of the sudden requirement, Ayan was given the keys, a warm hug, and a delicious meal, during which he was updated about everything happening in the family. He shifted to his new home at the beginning of the second year of college. The apartment had two rooms, a hall, and a tiny balcony. It had windows in every room. Ayan chose the one with a view of the tiny garden. In the garden, he saw a tiny lemon plant growing alone as if someone loved it dearly and kept it away from bad company. He locked the other room, as it was of no use; and also as he had no intention of keeping another person in his house under any circumstances. Soon his room was filled with books, and the walls seemed to hide behind them. He bought speakers for his computer and listened to music all the time.

There was one thing that bothered him immensely– the response of the publishers. He had approached many publishers after the completion of his novel, but none of them seemed to be interested in his project. There were many reasons for this: first, because his novel was a complicated one; second, international publishers didn't respond to him; third, he wasn't ready to edit anything. But his fears and uncertainty were greatly neutralized by the walks he shared with Anna, as with those walks he had found a source of happiness; of recognition.

He was sitting on the couch he had placed right in front of the window, staring at the plant, then at the sky, and smoking when the door bell of his house rang. "It's open," he shouted but the bell rang again.

"I guess it's not," he said to himself, walked to the door and opened it to find Anna standing with her face red like a balloon about to burst. She walked straight into his room, while he stood at the door with a confused look. Anna and Mezz were the only frequent visitors at Ayan's place and also the ones who were allowed.

"Do you want coffee?" Ayan asked. She didn't reply but sat in furious anger. "You had a fight with him again?" he asked, sitting on the couch.

"He has started to abuse me! What is wrong with him? He abused me today." She said, with a look expressing extreme disgust. Ayan sat quietly with no response.

"I should make the coffee," he said, jumping up but stopped immediately noticing tears in her eyes. He stood beside the couch glancing at her for only a moment, after which he moved directly into the kitchen to prepare coffee. He could hear her sob but she didn't break down. After a while, when the coffee was ready, he came back to the room with a mug in his left hand and a cigarette in his right. "There," he said, keeping the coffee mug on the desk and sat back on the couch next to the window.

"Do you have anything with which I could wipe my face?" she asked, her voice breaking due to her sobbing.

"Nope," Ayan answered. "I don't expect anyone to cry here." He turned to her, "and certainly not my friends." He paused and looked straight again. "What have you read in History?" he asked.

She didn't answer but coughed.

"Any war?" he asked. "You must have, maybe you are finding it problematic to remember right now. You have heard of World War II, haven't you? Do you know how many people died? Of course you don't, but do you know how they died? Ever heard of Auschwitz? Concentration camps? People were gassed alive; taken as prisoners and then experimented on. Let me tell you a little something about it." He paused. "There were special types of experiments conducted on twins in Auschwitz, the objective was to find the secrets of heredity. They believed that if the German women could give birth to twins–who were blue eyed and had blonde hair, the future would be secured. These experiments were conducted under the guidance of a Doctor, named Josef Mengele. You see, as the prisoners used to arrive in Auschwitz, they were sent either to hard labor or to the gas chamber, and being one of the many selectors, Mengele had given strict instructions to the SS not to miss any twins, and when the twins were found they were taken away from their parents." Ayan took a puff of his cigarette.

"Of course it was a tough choice for the parents to decide whenever the SS shouted *zwillinge* (twins), as they had no idea if it was good or bad to be a twin. Around three thousand twins were taken, and most of them were kids. Now after they had been taken, they were kept in separate twin barracks, given showers and breakfasts, and often in the mornings, Mengele would arrive with a pocket full of candies and chocolates for the children. He would play with them, and was called Uncle Mengele out of affection." He took another puff.

"And then one day, the experiments began: all the twins had to have their blood drawn, in large quantities, obviously for experiments, daily." He emphasized the last word. "And because the little children's arms and hands were very small, blood was drawn from their necks. Trucks would come to take those whose numbers were called to laboratories where several experiments were conducted on them. To develop the ability to create blue eyes, several chemicals and injections were put in their eyes, which would often lead to blindness and many other similar painful effects. Mysterious injections were put into their spines and spinal taps with no anesthesia. Diseases like typhus and tuberculosis were purposely infused. Surgeries like organ removal, castrations, and amputations were done without anesthesia. And on those who used to die, autopsies were the next experiment conducted on their bodies."

Anna interrupted, deeply disturbed by the images that were generating in her mind from Ayan's words, "Why are you telling me all of this? Stop it."

Ayan looked at her calmly and spoke, "Let me quote someone who was there," and he picked up a book from the many that were kept on the floor in a pile "I cannot tell you how I felt. It is impossible to put in words how I felt. They had taken away my father, my mother, my two older brothers, and now my twin." He paused and said, "It's written by Moshe Offer." He kept the book back in its place. "Now what do you understand?" he asked.

Anna was confused, and remained quiet.

"I am talking about the history of tears," Ayan said. "Do you know any child? Imagine such a thing happening to that kid. And if you can't, take your dad. Can you think of such a thing happening to your dad? Or simply picture yourself being separated from your mom and dad forever by the claws of death? All those kids who died in the camps had parents. Can you picture what their parents must have felt till the time they were alive? You want to know what I think? They must have cried a lot. Such are the losses that have made way for tears to come out; What is your loss? Why are you crying?"

Anna understood what he was saying and remained quiet.

He continued, "The reason you can cry, laugh, dance, or celebrate at this moment, is a gift given to you by people. Do you know how many soldiers died in World War II? Americans, Russians, British? What did they die for? For honor, respect, or medals? They are dead, so obviously they didn't die for their own good. Then for whom did they die? They died for you– people you don't remember any more and you hate studying about." He paused.

"Do you know why child marriages were so prevalent during the Mughal period? Because the Mughal clan leaders used to pick girls from the streets if they liked them, but left the married women alone. The rules stated that women were prohibited to dance, to roam about in the streets, to open their hair or face, and what not. You are living in a place where all these rules do not exist, where we have a free will, where you are free to lead your life in whichever way you want, because people gave their lives to change it. Have you read about the Indian Freedom struggle? There are countless things that aren't given in the course books because of the horror of such events. So, don't ever cry in your life. Cherish this time you are born in, and always remember the fact that people died for the free air you breathe, a free will that you have. Remember the worth of your tears and let them out when you truly know what sorrow is." He paused, looking at her, "Don't ever cry, not for yourself, but in respect for those who didn't even have the choice to love."

She sat quietly listening to each and every word that came out of his mouth, and stopped crying. Her face was still red but she was not angry any more.

"Now tell me, why did he abuse you?" Ayan asked calmly.

Anna hesitated and then said, "because I told him that I am not in love with him anymore."

Ayan kept quiet and then assured her, "I am sure everything will be fine between both of you." Listening to this, Anna looked at him with contempt. "I have to go," she said rising up from the chair, and noticing that he made no attempt to stop her, she left.

Ayan lit up another cigarette. "Disappointing," he said.

The next day, she didn't come to the college. After the classes, as he was walking back to his house, he received a call from her. "Hey!" he said, picking up the call.

"Hi! How are you doing?" Anna responded.

"I am good. Where are you?"

"Actually, I am just.... I didn't feel like coming," she said hesitatingly.

"Is everything alright?" Ayan asked, getting a feeling that something was wrong.

"Yes yes. Just wanted to talk to you for a while."

"Sure, You want me to come to your hostel. We can go for coffee," Ayan offered.

"No, please. It's okay, I am okay."

"Anna," Ayan said, "look if you want to talk, like you said a moment ago, we can meet and talk; but if you don't, then what are we doing right now?"

"I just wanted to talk to you on the phone," she said. "Just have a small conversation. Anyway, I have to go now. Bye." And she hung up which confused as well as infuriated Ayan. He took an auto-rickshaw and came to his home, threw his stuff in the corner, opened the computer and played Beethoven's Symphony 7, in full volume, then went to the bathroom where he submerged his head in a bucket full of water– an action attributed as one of the causes that lead to Beethoven's deafness–to cool himself down.

He sat in front of his desk and started to type:

> You have summarized the greatest potential you have in yourself into the weakest assumptions and improvisations that mark nothing else but pretension–which is the sole cause of your living.
>
> Small talk, as I would define, is another term for an appropriate amount of time, bundled together for the release of the unconscious desires of the smart man, and the conscious and willing desires of laymen to share inability, comfort, and thoughtlessness, as small talks unravel neither the state of mind of a person nor the state of action.

He lit up a cigarette, walked to the window to see the plant, and thought about Sara after a long time. He went back and took out the notebook from a box which read on its cover, *A Thousand Letters*. He smiled as he opened the notebook, took a pen, and started writing:

9 May, 2006

Dearest,
What I hold profound with the deepest respect, is the picture of you embedded in my heart, in the safest, purest corner of my truly mechanized, advancing, adapting, constantly changing self. If I were wounded by a thousand thorns, it would still be nothing in comparison to the pain I silently infuse every time I close my eyes to remember you, my love.

Tears have long forgotten their role, and loneliness seems to be the pleasant belonging I cherish the most. I wish I could spend a night with you, and not in any desired form, but because I feel night is the truth. I wish sometimes I could have been more important to you; or be a part that you would allow to stay nearby.

He withdrew his hand from writing further as the bell rang, he quickly closed the notebook and secreted it underneath the disarranged pile of books kept on the floor. The bell rang again, and he finally went to the door and opened it for Anna.

"Hi, Ayan," she said in a soft voice that expressed vulnerability. Her face was red, her hair was untidy as if done in haste, and she wore black sunglasses and a cap with her usual dress – a black tee and shorts.

"Come in," Ayan said and closed the door behind her. He noticed that her lower lip was swollen. "Anna, show me your face." He focused on her lips, and noticed a deep cut on the left side of her lower lip. "How did you hurt yourself?" he asked.

"Just an accident. It was a friend's fingernail," she said, throwing away the topic and starting a new one. "Ayan, I wanna talk to you about something."

"Sure." he said, sitting on the couch.

She sat on the single bed, "I can't hide anything from you anymore," she said, "I believe you are entitled to know everything. The reason why I have been having so many fights with my boyfriend is you. I have waited too long to see if you feel this way too but I can't wait any longer. What I told him yesterday was not that I am not in love with him anymore; it was that I am in love with you. He said that he wanted to meet for the last time, so we met today to end things. And we broke up."

"And that is when he hit you?" Ayan interrupted, and his words brought the tears in her eyes, rolling down her cheeks.

She spoke in an angry tone, "Ayan, you don't have a clue about what I had to go through everyday pretending to be in love with somebody, being guided and told to do so by a person whom I actually love. Every day I used to think maybe I am wrong; maybe it's because of your intellect that I am confusing admiration with love. Every time he tried to touch me, I used to have a sickening feeling, and every time when I was close to you, I never wanted to leave. How could I have let him touch me? And for that, he hit me. Oh God." And she broke down crying but recollected herself immediately without the help of Ayan.

"Look, I can't be friends with you any more if you don't love me," she said, wiping off her tears. "I am not asking you for anything right now. Think as much as you want to, and then simply message me your answer." She stood up and started to leave, but Ayan called her name and stopped her. "Anna, wait!" He stood, looking at her with a confused look. "Get yourself a band-aid for that cut," he said, pointing at his own lips.

"Thanks for your concern," she said, and left. Ayan took out his phone and called Mezz. He didn't pick up. Ayan messaged him to call back as soon as possible. He did call after an hour. "Hey, where were you?"

"I had a class," Mezz replied. "This second year is going crazy. Whats up with you? And what's with that girl Anna. I have a missed call from her."

"She called you?" Ayan asked, surprised.

"Yeah. Why? What happened?"

"I really need your advice," Ayan said. "So, get your ass here as soon as you can."

"Well," Mezz said, "I am not doing anything right now. Studies are not important at all; you are right. I am on my way." And he hung up.

During the meeting, Ayan explained the entire situation to Mezz. They both sat quietly, thinking about the best solution in order to restore the natural balance that had existed before. "I had anticipated something like this but her boyfriend smacking her, that's a bummer. You wanna do something about it?" Mezz asked.

"Well, what do you suppose could be an apt response to irrationality and violence?" Ayan asked.

"Non-violence?" Mezz replied in a confused manner.

Ayan looked at him with a twisted expression and said, "ignorance, in this case. Only if he is finally satisfied and would prefer to stay out of her life."

"What about the girl?" Mezz asked.

"I don't know. I really don't know what to do."

"I don't understand why you are not interested in dating her," Mezz inserted, curiously.

"I can't! It would be lying to myself."

"Yes yes, you love Sara. But what is so wrong in trying?" Mezz broke the silence again.

"Trying what?" Ayan asked.

"To be in a relationship."

"I don't have any reason to," Ayan replied sternly.

"So the question is, what is it that will get you into a relationship?"

"What are you getting at?" Ayan said, staring at him.

"Look, what do you understand by a relationship?" Mezz asked. "If you date this girl, or any girl, you don't become her father. What I mean is: you don't incur her responsibility for life. If you mess up, you mess up."

Ayan remained quiet, contemplating his words in his mind. Mezz resumed: "Do you know any of her friends?"

"She has a group of friends." Ayan said. "They are all her school buddies, so I have never met any of them. Do you think she is bluffing with this clause?" Ayan asked, suspiciously.

"Of either being lovers or not friends at all?" Mezz asked and Ayan nodded in response. "Look, I would be glad to tell you that it's a bluff, but she is not a guy. Girls don't bluff. This is not a bluff. If you care about this chick, take this seriously," Mezz said.

"But I don't love her," Ayan said in a thoughtful manner. "That was the point of telling her I am gay. What happened to that?"

Mezz laughed. "Dude, you have to build a story for that, and it doesn't end at telling her that you are gay. You have to continuously make her remember the fact by getting into that character; give her a reason for stuff like why you are not dating anyone right now, and talk about a lot of crap, which I am sure you didn't do because you can't."

"I don't love her. I think I should message her that," Ayan said.

"But before you do," Mezz said, "did you know that her father owns a publishing house?"

Ayan looked at him confused, and cried, "What?"

"Her father owns a publishing house– you know, for fiction novels and non-fiction."

"How do you know that?" Ayan asked quickly.

"Remember when those guys stopped you in the park, I told you that very day that I will get every detail about this girl."

"Why didn't you tell me about it?" Ayan asked.

"I forgot. But now I remember. If you let this chick go, you are ruining your chances of getting your novel published."

Ayan remained in shock for a minute. He cried, "You said you knew it would come to this, but didn't expect that he would hit her. So, you knew she was going to fall for me?" he asked.

"Dude, everyone knew except you."

"Who is everyone here?"

"It's just a figure of speech. Listen, if I had told you that her father owns or works in a reputed publishing house, you would have talked to her, and your novel would have been published."

"And is that bad?" Ayan asked in surprise.

"No, of course not," Mezz replied, "it can still be published. You just have to say yes. What I mean is, if you had told her about it earlier, she would have done this as a favour for her friend; but right now, you have lost that favour. Right now, you can either be her boyfriend and regain it, or be f…ed."

Ayan was in deep shock at this moment. He said, "So,

all of this is happening because of you. You planned all of this!" He shook his head and started laughing.

"The bet is just an excuse, dude." Mezz explained. "What I really want; why I really did this is because I want you to move on now. Sara is gone. We don't know where she is or about her future plans? With whom she is right now? Who knows if she is committed and has found a guy who loves her just as much as you do? And maybe all of this is wrong, and both of you are meant to be together, but such a tiny possibility does not imply that you can't date anyone else. And you know why? Because it's delusional. And Anna is worth a shot. I mean, I have never seen you spending so much time with any other girl. I am not telling you that she is the one. This is a trial. This is an experience whose beauty you can only find by living it. Give it a chance."

Chapter - 13

The emperor asked, "Who are you?"

The man replied in a feeble tone, "I am Eklavya."

"Who do you think I am?"

"You are the emperor; you are all-knowing and the wisest of all, my lord."

"Wrong," the emperor said. "I am nothing. We all live in nothingness. Erase every idea, every thought you have formed of yourself from your mind, because if you won't, then I can't teach you anything, you have already placed yourself somewhere."

"Tell me, how would you feel if I applauded your work?" The emperor asked.

"I would feel glad, my lord." The man answered, hesitatingly.

"And how would you feel if I proclaimed you as the wisest man I have ever known?"

"It would be a dream come true."

"Is it what you want?" The emperor asked. "What if my inspiration behind proclaiming you as such, is only to infuse motivation in you? What if there is no such thing in the world as the wisest? What if you were to find that we are mere specks of lives and whatever you achieve is nothing? But if, by any certain chance, I do proclaim you as the wisest, then I am only infusing in you vices, such as pride, arrogance, and superiority over those whom I compare you to. Then I, myself, am a fool, to have divided humans into classes in your eyes, so you can look down on them with unworthiness. But the question is: do you think your mind is gullible to such vices?"

The man answered, "No."

"Then answer my questions. What is the spirit of a man?" The emperor asked.

"Hope."

"What is pain?"

"Learning."

"What is the reason to live?"

"Evaporation of life from our physical body to abstraction by finding the universal truth."

"What is the meaning of life?"

"Evolution, in each step until it meets destruction."

"What is love?"

"The soul of a man."

"What is inspiration?" He asked sternly.

"God."

"What is truth?"

"Suffering."

"And what is the universal truth?"

"It's a series of realizations that true happiness is not in earning, it's in giving. That life in itself is a fight against evil, and submitting yourself to any cause against it, which, for a moment might appear meaningless, can change the world. That every man shall help those in need to extents that may surpass the desires which limit such an act. That if you accept death, it can't kill you, but if you won't, its fear will, everyday." Eklavya answered.

"And do you know any such men?" The emperor asked.

"The prophets sent by God."

"Why do you place them amongst men?"

"Like you said, we are mere specks of life,

regardless of how great or epoch-making one might become. Even the prophets sent by God lived the very fate of a man."

Ayan stopped his fingers from typing more and paused. He stood up and walked to the window, from where he looked at the lemon plant. And for a moment, he closed his eyes and reminisced the recent events.

His novel had been published only a few days ago. It happened because of the help offered by Anna's father, which was the result of Anna's vigorous persuasion, leading to a brief interview of Ayan by her father that ended with these lines:

"What is your true purpose to write?" Her father asked, sipping whisky from his glass. Ayan thought for a while, and answered, "I write to create new lives to create an effect amongst the true living."

After his novel was published, he engaged himself in writing again, but wasn't satisfied with the outcome. Actually there were many reasons and new developments that had kept him occupied, the most important being his relationship with Anna. They had been seeing each other for four months now, and in that time, Ayan witnessed a steady decline in reading, contemplating, writing, and finding time for himself, which consequently made him more restless–something that he didn't share with Anna. As a result, he subconsciously tried to satisfy himself by writing more and more whenever he got time.

Another recent development that bothered him was their sexual relationship. He had never planned for such an eventuality to occur for the fulfillment of his desires; and each day, as he submitted himself to lust, he pondered more and more about the psychological reasons attached to it, and with the help of his findings, he explored the secrets of lust. He thought about the relationship between love and sex, and later on, concluded that both have no connection with each other at all. In his writings, he never opposed the idea of sexual relationships, even though having already stated lust as one of the prime roots of evil.

With time, he had stopped writing letters to Sara. The letters, as well as the notebook (A Thousand Letters) were hidden somewhere in the dark, buried inside a box, far away from any remembrance in his mind. Although he did write letters to Anna, but not the kind which he wrote to Sara, not that he didn't try, but was unable to due to the absence of love. He started to write her letters that were restricted to what the exact moment and the surroundings had to offer respectively. The most recent letter that he had written was a direct outcome of an immense downpour, the pedestrians, and the perfect spot that made him an eye-witness to the exact moment.

18 September, 2006

Anna,

Apparently, this is a crazy moment. What is it about life; that we so gladly choose to speak about it only in selfishly intentional and biased moments, desperately claiming to involve only and only sense!

Where does sense lie? This is my question.

Does it constantly find a new position with the different human-minds' understanding of reason?

Or is it in the parallel co-existence of the unconscious with the inner voice?

Or is it in the following of the human heart, regardless of the causes or repercussions?

Well, sense does seem to find a different definition with the plurality of human existence. Perhaps, there is no sense in tomorrow, just as there can't be any absolute sense in living a life. Even when you perform actions, things that are outside the circumscribed perimeter of your manipulation/control still occur and affect you.

What is sin?

Any sort of wrong-doing that might hurt others or hurt your own self?

I wonder: Is perfection the absence of sin, or is it something else entirely?

I do not dwell in the illusions of perfection. Sin can't be aptly defined as wrong, if it contains a will and an action to explore the truth.

He was waiting for Anna, sipping tea from a little Chinese cup, sitting on the couch in his room, and thinking about writing another novel. The reviews about his currently published novel had appeared to be fair and remarkably satisfying for both the publishing house and Ayan himself. He was moderately affected and impressed by the effect his novel had had in his college campus, as he was now the talk of the town, with opposing and contradictory views being exhibited from various corners. Many people even doubted his capability to produce such thoughts that were talked about in the book, and held that they might have occurred to him by mistake. What he wanted to write was hidden under an ambiguity of some sort–such were the thoughts of his competitors, men older to him, and men who believed they were smarter than him. All of them were silenced after the success of his second novel which not only became an International best-seller but also offered much greater scope of thought.

After Ayan had finished the tea, the door bell rang and he opened it for Anna. The moment she entered the house, she was welcomed by music. "What are you listening to?" She asked about music for the first time.

"Classical music," he answered, picking up the cup, and moved to the kitchen to make coffee for her, knowing without asking that she would not have tea.

"Why do you always keep listening to that? Don't you get bored of it?" She asked nonchalantly, inspecting the things that were kept on his desk, not realizing the gravity of her simple plain comment.

"I listen to it because this is music," he said, emphasizing his last words. He wanted to give a more extensive reply, involving sarcasm and insult to her choice of music, but suppressed his anger. She was picking up papers and randomly going through them, "Ayan, what is OP?" Anna asked, loud enough for him to be able to hear.

"Op?" Ayan said. "Opus? It's Latin for work. It means a work of art. Are you checking out the list of music?"

"I just have this paper," she replied, "there are so many names written on it. Op. 24, Op. 32, and so many weird long names."

"Yeah," he said from the kitchen. "Those are names of composers. Great musicians." He whispered the last two words and waited for the coffee to be ready, as he didn't want to go into the room and face her at this moment. After the coffee was prepared, he came and served it to her. "Did you read any of the books I told you to?" he asked.

"I tried reading the Machiavelli one."

"Well, very good. And?"

"I don't know; I didn't like it."

"How much did you read?"

"Few pages," she replied.

"You didn't even read the full book."

"I was bored. It was boring! Come on! I am entitled to have an opinion, am I not?" She protested.

He sat down quietly, looking at her and thinking.

"You haven't read any of the books, but you have time for everything else?"

"Everything else? Like what?" Her tone became serious.

"You can't figure that out?" he asked. "Think! What did you do last night?"

"I was tired, so I slept," she replied. "God! I cannot work like you do."

"Before that. Before you slept. What did you do?"

"I was out with my friends?" Anna said. "It was Sakshi's birthday!" She looked at him, expecting him to understand the degree of urgency the occasion required.

"I don't know who that is!" he said.

"You've met her," she complained. "It's your problem you don't remember my friends."

"They are not worthy of being remembered."

"Yes, everyone I know is stupid, including me. And you are a genius! Happy?" She said in an offended tone.

"That is the reason you got tired last night." He said, unaffected by her previous statements. "You go out with your friends almost every day, and the occasions are simply idiotic. But do I ever stop you from hanging out with them? What I ask from you is to read–for me, if not for yourself. You went to her birthday party because of friendship; you can't read a book for the person you love?"

She sighed, "Ayan, it's not that I didn't try. I couldn't. I am sorry."

"I am sorry, and?" he asked.

"What do you expect me to do?" She asked in an irritated tone. "I am trying. I can't force myself, and if I can, I won't. Please!"

Ayan remained quiet after that statement. "Your coffee is getting cold," he said.

He felt extreme irritation accumulating in his chest,

but tried to breathe it out slowly. The single emotion that reigned on top of everything at the moment was the realization of a strange fault: that this was a wrong decision.

After she finished her coffee, she came closer to Ayan and hugged him tightly. “I am sorry I didn't read the book. Forgive me baby, please?” She said in a childish tone.

Ayan knew that he would have to forgive her eventually. He looked into her eyes, and knew that it wasn't her fault. They both smiled and kissed each other, and gently made love on the couch, and from the couch moved to the bed where they took a nap. In the evening, Anna left and Ayan took off for a walk. Bored, he called Mezz.

“Hey! What are you doing?”

“Working. What's up with you?”

“Got time for a smoke?”

“I don't smoke. Are you coming?”

“I am bored, and I want to talk to you about something related to Anna,” Ayan said.

“Well, come to my hostel then,” Mezz suggested.

“Fine, I'm on my way.”

Chapter - 14

When he reached Mezz's hostel, he walked to his room, knocked at the door, and Rishabh opened it. Mezz was lying on the floor with a pile of books kept on either side of his head, that hid his face from anyone who entered through the door. The room gave an impression of a crime scene. "What's with the room?" Ayan asked. "That's how he lives," Rishabh said, sitting comfortably in one corner on a cushion, shuffling some papers.

Mezz got up. "Manners survive only in the realm of dignity," he said, "and a man loses dignity at the first sight of fear, threat, danger, lust, or any sort of calamity that circumstances might throw at him. It's a pretension, like wearing tight dresses to look attractively civilized."

He looked at Rishabh and asked, "Tell me, if a bomb dropped on your head right now, would you care about manners? Or would you care about survival? And, if I may ask: what do you think is more important?" Hearing no answer, he continued, "A man's true identity reveals itself in chaos, in destruction, which is why strife is the only truth. And that makes happiness an illusion, an inflated idea of fantasy confused with reality, okay Rishabh?"

"Yeah yeah, right!" Rishabh answered, going through the papers in his hands. Mezz stood up and stretched his body. "What's up with you?" he asked Ayan.

Ayan took out a cigarette from the pack, lit it, and opened the windows of the room. "I am kind of stuck between thoughts.".

"So, there are two thoughts?" Mezz said, in a playful manner.

Ayan said, "What do you understand of silence?"

"Silence as in quietness? Isolation?"

"No, no. Amongst men." Ayan corrected.

"Well, if you want to find the least foolish person in a group of fools, look for the one who is most silent." Mezz said.

"That's an interesting observation," Ayan said and took a deep puff on his cigarette. "Silence is a blank which we fill in accordance with our priorities: it's what we want the other person to understand. After all, it's human tendency to express and seek emotional approval, and silence fulfils this very requirement in the form of the willingness to listen. And that is how it becomes so misguiding. You understand me?"

"A little bit," Mezz answered.

"I have made a big mistake," Ayan said. "This was a mistake, Mezz. Remember; you said that it's not my responsibility? Well, she did become my responsibility, and now I am standing in the middle of time and my plans."

"Tell me what happened clearly —everything," Mezz said.

He immediately let it out, "You see, when we were friends, there were so many things that didn't require any unfolding or mentioning, although they were the most important things in her life; for example, I didn't know her friends, and I didn't care to know about them either; but after the relationship, it became important, and not only important–somehow mandatory."

"Did you meet them?" Mezz asked.

"Yeah, she made me."

"How was it?" he said.

After a moment's thought, Ayan said, "They are fine, with whatever they are doing. But we had no common interests to talk about. All they talked about, was wealth, cars, gadgets, and moral depravity. Surprisingly the only thing that did intrigue me was that they remembered the price of every car, cell phone, or any f…thing that is made to show off."

Mezz chuckled. "Did you notice anyone in that group

even moderately interested in Anna?"

"Amorously?" Ayan asked.

"Yeah."

"Well, why would someone with amorous inclinations towards Anna, show it in front of me?"

"Never trust people," Mezz said, "You never know. Anyway, after her friends, then what?"

"You know what I just figured out?" Ayan said with an expression of sudden realization. "It's because of expectations this relationship is getting ruined. And it all goes back to silence again."

"What do you mean?" Mezz asked, trying to understand.

Ayan explained, "when we used to take those walks in the park, I took her silence as a willingness to learn. And the more I taught her, the stronger this idea became that she is interested in being an intellectual. You see, I am a victim of the illusions of the power of speech. Whatever I taught her certainly was interesting and amusing and captivating, and it continued to have similar effect on her until it became monotonous for her mind. And her primary instincts–those which she had been ignoring all this while-finally emerged and took over the effects of my power of speech. Therefore, not even knowledge can cure mediocrity."

"So, is her mediocrity the problem?" Mezz asked.

"No, of course not," Ayan answered. "I don't judge people on their intellect. She's a nice human being. The problem is the foundation of my expectations. Because we had such a beginning, the idea which was in my mind, that attracted me towards the companionship, was born out of this mentality. It's not her fault. She was simply being a good listener. It's I who thought that she wanted to learn, when all she wanted was to listen. And this little mistake has messed me up." He looked at Mezz for sympathy.

"Now, I didn't know that she goes to late night parties, and when I asked her: 'why do you waste so much of your time?' She replied: 'don't worry, I don't do anything wrong in those parties.' Of course, I failed to find a correlation between her answer and my question, but I realized something: why the hell am I wasting my time?" Mezz laughed as he listened. "But then she calls me in the middle of the night, slightly drunk, and tells me that she is missing me, and I wonder what the apt response to this situation is. I tell her that I love her too; and you know what, Mezz? I am unable to work for the rest of the night because I am worried," Ayan said. By this time, Rishabh, who had kept the papers aside and was listening to Ayan carefully, joined Mezz in laughing at Ayan's situation.

Ayan continued, "This is only part one. There is a lot more but I don't want to start whining about everything. The thing is, after all of this, I look at her face, and I know it's not her fault. And I know that she wouldn't understand it even if I explain it to her. It's again the power of speech versus her instincts, in which I already know that I am going to lose eventually." He stopped.

"These are the most dangerous people in the world. Do you know why, Rishabh?" Mezz asked.

"Why?" Rishabh asked quickly being entertained by the discussion.

"For two reasons: one, because it hurts a lot when a loved one fucks you up; second, because they do so unknowingly, as a loved one would never deliberately do that. In this case, what do you think Ayan is doing? He is protecting her by not revealing what he is going through. But we have to dissect the problem here; what does she think she is doing? She is aimlessly hanging out with her friends. She does not understand the implications of her actions before she commits them. And the worst part is, she doesn't think about her boyfriend who actually has a life, is focused, and has an aim. How is she dangerous, Rishabh?" Mezz asked.

Rishabh looked at Ayan, and confidently said, "she doesn't understand the value of time, which is nothing for her, but everything to her boyfriend."

"Beautiful, Rishabh!" Mezz exclaimed.

"She doesn't understand the value of time," Mezz looked at Ayan, chuckling, "Who could have thought that? I am so proud of you, Rishabh. Now tell us your suggestions to solve this problem."

"I think they should talk about it openly. I am sure she would understand." He suggested, and Mezz looked at Ayan waiting for a reaction.

Ayan looked at Rishabh and said, "I am not saying that there isn't any place for amendments. But I ask you, is it my responsibility? If I am changing her, or at least trying to, then it clearly means that I am not in love with her. And even if I convince myself that it's the right thing to do, to change her, then why hadn't she ever tried to achieve anything before I met her?"

"The most important question is: do you love her?" Mezz asked.

Ayan paused for a while, and said, "compared to the love for Sara, not even close."

"Then what do you want?" Mezz asked.

"To end this relationship," Ayan answered.

"Are you sure?"

Ayan hesitated and murmured, "I don't know. It seems to be the only solution left."

"A man finds only what he wants to see," Mezz said. "There are no accidents, Ayan; everything is the result of the mindless, inanimate progression of time. If you are looking for flaws, then that's what you are going to find in everything. Look deep into your heart. What is it that you really want from this girl?"

"I don't love her. I never did. I have made many mistakes in the name of experiments, hope, excuses, and what not. But I can only say, that when I entered this relationship, I entered with an open mind, to accept whatever may come. And if this is what it has come down to, then I shall work in accordance with it."

"Okay, satisfactory!" Mezz said. "How do you plan to break up with her?" He asked.

"I was hoping you might help me with this," Ayan said.

"Look, a clean break-up is a challenge," Mezz explained. "Your prime focus is to save time, and break-ups can get messy. You might think that if you explain everything to her, she would understand, and of course she will. But again, your prime focus is to save time. It's the reason why you are breaking up with her in the first place. Now, if you break up in the conventional way; like having a mature talk about it, it could go smoothly, but then she will ask you to remain friends. You would agree to that because that sounds reasonable, and you are not a bad person. I mean, you are looking out for everyone's best interests here. Just think." He continued, "how does breaking up with her and then becoming friends afterwards, change anything? You are not fed up of the relationship, but her. You haven't realized that because it hasn't touched the peak of your tolerance yet. You are breaking up with her because she is stupid; and you didn't realize that until you came to know her completely. And that is why there is no scope for any friendship. If you stay friends, this problem won't be solved. I mean, she is in your class, and all the habits she has acquired such as clinging to you, spending time in your house, talking to you about stuff, coming to you with her problems–these things won't just disappear."

"You are right." Ayan agreed thoughtfully.

Mezz continued, "The first step is to realize, which you have, and the second is to isolate yourself from such distractions. And a clean break-up is a challenge, the question is: how to do it?

For a permanent solution, what you have to do is: do not break up with her, make her break up with you, so there is no guilt. In that way, she is not sad because she thinks that she has made the right decision, and is therefore satisfied. In such break-ups, the chance to become friends arises after months when the anguish has ended. How do you do that? You can cheat on her, but that involves a lot of drama, and the possibility of getting slapped." Ayan interrupted Mezz's dialogue, "Just get to the point."

"Okay, fine!" he said. "Tell me, what is the most prevalent reason behind any conflict?"

"Ego," Ayan answered.

"What is the thing that man loves the most?" he asked.

"Self."

"There is only one thing that conquers love: self love," Mezz said. "From now on, don't suppress what you feel or want to say. On the contrary, exaggerate. Do not insult, but inform. Tell her the truth. Tell her how stupid her actions are, at every chance you get. She will break up with you within a week without any tears or words of grief."

It didn't take a week, but two months for Ayan and Anna to finally end the relationship. After their break-up, Anna took an Internship in Mumbai and disappeared for a month. When she returned, neither of them endeavored to be friends. As time passed, many rumours about Anna flew in the air. They were forgotten, or often replaced by new rumours; but the truth was, she didn't date anyone for two months after her split with Ayan. Finally, after a long time, she got into a relationship with an old friend, who had secretly been in love with her for many years.

In the last year of his college, the year 2007, Ayan engaged himself in writing his second novel: about a brilliant psychologist, who tries to understand the connection of mind with spirituality and meditation by taking a journey to self-awakening. He called it: '*The memoirs of awakening*'. After he finished writing the book, he submitted the manuscript to only a few publishers, and was accepted by all of them, even though he finally had to choose one. During this period of time, he had almost forgotten Anna, as he hardly attended the college in the last year, and nor did she.

It was an important year for all of them. Mezz had started training under a lawyer, and was learning from many other sources; therefore was far too busy. It had become impossible for both the friends to meet, because of the amount of work they had dedicated themselves to; but they often exchanged messages and talked to each other on the phone.

In the year 2008, Ayan's second novel made the best-selling list of a significantly eminent newspaper for many months in India. And as time progressed, many more newspapers and magazines and websites followed, and his novel received not only national but International praise. This development greatly accelerated the sales of his first novel too, making him wealthier as he hadn't put any of the accumulating money into any use apart from basic necessities. As more time passed, he had to do interviews with magazines, websites, and newspapers, which he began to find annoying and intolerable due to the lack of good questions, and the quality of minds that interviewed him.

In the year 2009, he went to Mumbai for a book signing of his second novel at a book-store, where he met Sara.

Chapter - 15

Sara opened her eyes, and noticed the ceiling fan. She turned over on her right, and noticed two laptops and some food kept on the little round table. She got her legs out of the blanket and firmly put them down on the ground. The region the blanket now covered stretched between her chest and her thighs. She yawned again and sat there for a minute, thinking about making a cup of coffee for herself, and then properly arranging the room.

A male voice came from behind her, "Sara, could you make some coffee, please?"

"Yeah, sure," she replied, picking up her shorts that

were lying on the floor, and also her tee and her underwear. The person who was sleeping on the left side of the bed was Sara's third lover, after her split with Nilay.

Sara and Nilay lived together for a year, in an apartment which belonged to Nilay. During that time, certain changes in both their behaviors changed the presupposed fate of their relationship. Nilay had become very irritable, after a part of his mind accepted that he had lost his freedom by sharing an apartment with Sara. Previously, when he lived with his male friends, or alone, he had the privilege of talking to anyone he wanted–which mainly meant his ex-lover. But there were restrictions imposed naturally by Sara's presence that gradually eroded the excitement that initially had driven him into making this decision. Also, Sara had read many messages on his phone of his ex-lover, which went far beyond the boundaries of a normal friendship.

After six months of their relationship, due to their increasing number of fights, they slept in different rooms, and many a time, Nilay spent the nights at his friends' places to avoid any further worsening of the situation. But in certain recurrent, love-filled nights, caused by some special occasion, they both re-united and made love and shared promises of being eternal lovers and never leaving each other. And the next morning a simple mishap would restore the previously shared turbulent state of no sex and mutual hatred.

Such an arrangement went on until finally one day,

Nilay accompanied by a few close friends, beat up one of Sara's friends–also her classmate–to an extent that he was hospitalized. He believed that either they were more than friends, or were beginning to become more than friends.

Sara broke up with Nilay at that point, shifted to a friend's place, and lived there for two months. As it turned out, Nilay's accusations against Sara were not absolutely false; on the contrary, they were true. She did have feelings for that friend of hers, Snehil. He was a tall young man, with long shabby hair. Apart from being a classmate of Sara's, Snehil was a painter, and had a very notorious reputation of courting women, about which she was completely oblivious.

Sara and Snehil became very close friends, as she held herself responsible for his situation, and he took maximum advantage of it. During the next three months, he sang her many famous romantic songs. Although he had sung the same songs to many women, but when he sang them to Sara, it appeared as if the beauty described in the songs, described her. They became very close, and after a while, Snehil too started liking her. On his birthday, he took her out to a video game parlour at a mall, where they spent the entire evening playing games. In the night, both of them took a long walk, and he kissed her before he left. That very night, she received a call from Nilay, and he told her everything about Snehil and his past relationships, and even gave Sara the phone numbers of the girls Snehil had abandoned. And that was the end of this relationship.

After the shock of finding the truth about Snehil, Sara went to Delhi for a month and a half, to do an internship at a newspaper. In the first week, she stayed mostly in her house, watched romantic films, and often cried alone. Nevertheless, she decided to take studies very seriously, and started reading books such as autobiographies, biographies, and literary works. She had scored the highest marks in the first year of college, and was determined to maintain similar academic scores in the coming years.

She joined a library nearby her house, as she hated reading books on her computer. She stayed in the library for most of the day, apart from the time she spent at the office and at her home. At the library there was a young man, who usually sat close to her and read Leo Tolstoy's *War and Peace*. Whenever Sara would start reading, she glanced at him for no reason, and found his eyes staring at the open book as if he was hypnotized.

One day, while she was reading *Mein Kampf*, she heard a voice behind her "Hello?" She turned around to find the same young man standing there, quite worried. "Can I use your phone, please? I really need to make an important call," he said softly.

"Sure! Here," she said, handing him the phone.

He dialled a number on her phone, and his phone rang simultaneously. "Got it. Thanks for your number," he said with a smile, kept her phone back on the table, and left. That evening, he sent her a message to apologize about stealing her number, and asked the names of her favorite writers. She didn't reply. At night, he called her, and sounded absolutely charming. He made funny remarks about the books he had noticed her reading, and then made some charming yet funny comments about her hair. The next day in the library, they sat next to each other, read more, and talked less. In the following days, they talked more and read less. After a week, they were consuming beverages and meals at different eating joints together.

Sameer was smarter than most of the people Sara had met in her life, and smarter than every boy she had dated. At this vulnerable phase of her life, when she desperately believed that she needed a true friend, one with whom she could share everything that had happened, Sameer's presence became special because of the maturity and understanding he possessed. As time passed, she told him everything about her past relationships. He remarked, thoughtfully, "You are looking for true love, maybe unknowingly. And people are going to take advantage of that because even the possibility of finding it, makes you vulnerable."

At the end of the month, he told her about his life, which was nothing but a chain of unfortunate events; and because of his story, she fell in love with him, confusing tragedy with altruism. In the first week of the second month, she confessed her love to him, and he told her that he loved her too. She was convinced that it was pure love, and would last forever. After her internship was over, she went back to Mumbai, and changed her apartment to live alone. They talked to each other for hours on the phone, and he suggested to her many books on many different subjects. He introduced her to the novels of Marcel Proust, Douglas Adams, George Orwell, and other writers, basically the novels that had inspired him. Sameer became the ideal man for Sara, and she loved him completely.

After two months, he came to Mumbai to meet her, and stayed at her apartment. He had already told her that he had a surprise for her, and after they met, he revealed the news that he had been selected to do his doctorate from a University in the UK. He put the choice in her hands to decide whether he should go or stay—a clever, diplomatic move which was meant to work in his favour. In the evening, both of them went for a stroll, and on their way back, dined at a Chinese restaurant close to Sara's apartment. At night, he took out a book from his bag, and presented it to her.

"Lethargic life of *Andrew Sen.*" Sara read the name of the novel.

"It's a brilliant book," he said. "It's about a guy whose name is Andrew Sen, and whenever he sleeps, he wakes up in a dream world. The novel is fantasy, psychological, philosophical, and it's mind blowing stuff. The dreams are not like the regular dreams that we have. They are very realistic, and each dream takes place in a distinct world. But the dream-worlds, they are weird. The thing is, whenever he wakes up in a dream, he is in a new world, and it's not some alien type stupid world, it's something really familiar to us, stuff that is in history. For example, in one dream, he wakes up during the French Revolution; in another dream, he is a writer who has locked himself in a room for days and is literally torturing his mind to write his best book. And the best part is in the last dream, when Andrew wakes up in the Garden of Eden, and has a conversation with the snake. That will blow your mind."

"Okay, so it's mainly fantasy, right?" Saraasked.

"No", he said. "Those are just plots so you can have, many changes, and different worlds, and different characters. Those are Andrew's dreams, but every dream basically has one philosophical question, whose answer Andrew Sen is finding, while being stuck in that particular situation. The novel basically has every philosophical question you can think of, and each chapter is dedicated to one, and the dream ends when he has found the answer."

"So, what's the end?" Sara asked.

"That is very predictable. He dies. But the novel is not about the story, it's about the content." Sameer explained.

"He dies in his dream?" Sara asked, confused.

"Of course not," Sameer said, chuckling, "he dies because the knowledge that he is obtaining from each dream is mind blowing, and he knows that his dreams are something special. So Andrew becomes obsessed with his knowledge and starts taking drugs to induce sleep, and then sleeps for hours to dream so he can obtain more knowledge. And if he is sleeping all the time, and not eating, or drinking, but taking more and more drugs, he is going to die." He paused to drink water, and continued, "It's there in the end, you know, when he wakes up after a dream, and looks into the mirror, and can't recognize his face. He is so thin and weak that he can't move. But he still doesn't care because he is filled with excessive pride, and the worlds that his dreams have provided him are so full of fascination that the real world begins to look unreal to him. And there is another perspective to it too," he added. "After he wakes up all thin and weak, the writer talks about another thing that is keeping him standing, other than pride, and it's the strength of knowledge, the energy of enlightenment. His body is so full of knowledge in that moment that it has left the earthly form and connected itself with the energy of the universe, or something like that."

"So how does he die if his body is functioning on the energy of the universe?" Sara questioned.

"It's just a thought. He is talking about positivity. Of course he is weak and pathetic and is going to die." Sameer said.

"It sounds good. Actually, it sounds interesting, ignoring the fact that I know the story," Sara said.

"Trust me; I haven't ruined anything for you. It's a treat. Read the reviews, they are awesome. And do you know one more thing?"

"What?"

"It's written by a guy your age," Sameer said.

"Nineteen?"

"Yep."

"Ayan." She read the name of the Author. "Why does it only have his first name?"

"I don't know," he said "He is in Delhi University. It's his first book."

"Wow, looks like I have made a mistake coming to Mumbai. You are in Delhi. He is in Delhi. I am from Delhi. All my favourite people are in Delhi," she said, throwing the book aside, and moving closer to Sameer.

They both kissed. After watching a French film and having pizzas, they switched off the lights and made love twice in the night, and once in the morning after they had woken up.

Within three months, Sameer shifted to the U.K. After that, the troubles started in their relationship as they barely talked on the phone, and the e-mails that they once rapidly exchanged gradually lessened in number. She took her exams at the end of the year. After a while, Sara received a long e-mail from Sameer, explaining that whatever they once shared wasn't working out for him anymore. He also wrote that they should find different partners and mentioned the fact that he had already found a lover for himself, which left her devastated. She cried the hardest in her life and thought of calling up every person she knew, except her parents.

It was the last year of her graduation, and she had been without a boyfriend for three months, when she received a love letter from a classmate of hers. In the letter, he had confessed to have loved her for the past three years. This fellow, who wrote her the letter, was not an interesting personality, and nowhere close to being even remotely equal to any of her formal lovers, in any aspect. Yet his letter made her believe in the writer's supposed true love as he had waited all these years, watching her throw herself into the arms of wrong men, and like a true lover, waiting for her to understand the true worth of his love. And it worked.

She was immediately attracted towards him, though not very impressed by his intellect, which is why his money had to make up for it. Ashish came from an immensely wealthy background. To make this obvious, he often changed cars, escorted her to the most expensive places, bought her almost everything she spoke about or unknowingly expressed that she had wanted and filled her apartment with expensive objects she didn't need. All these things did make her happy, but she was happier about the fact that he was crazily in love with her, and between them, she was the smarter and dominating one.

After a week, she told him that she loved him too. She was determined not to be amorously inclined towards any other man in the future, believing that love meant not finding the person you love, but finding the person who loves you. After a month, she left her apartment and shifted with him, as his apartment was bigger.

Ashish did not have a handsome personality. He was almost unattractive, and his appearance projected vanity, as if there was nothing else that he wanted the other person to know about him but the fact that he was rich.

He had a group of friends, who flattered him at all times, but flattered him most when anyone of them needed one of his cars, or needed his money. For example, he was the one who paid whenever they consumed alcohol, drugs, or enjoyed the services of prostitutes, which basically summed up their lives. But Ashish didn't have as many bad habits as his friends did. He was addicted to many types of drugs, consumed alcohol everyday, lent his money to anyone with a sad face and a sob story and forgot about it. Regardless of all these things, Sara loved him, because he loved her back. The truth was: she had a plan. She believed that at one point she would make him realize that his friends were using him for monetary benefits, and also ruining his life. What she didn't realize was that he didn't have any plans at all.

After the final year of her college was over, Sara went to Delhi and had a conversation with her parents regarding her future plans, as they had naturally assumed that she would be applying to some foreign university for her Masters in History. This conversation–which was supposed to remind her of the fact that she hadn't made any plans—turned out to be a fruitless one, as Sara explained that she wanted to stay in Mumbai, and look for a job. Her father was not satisfied with her answers, and understood immediately that she had lost her focus because of a romantic relationship. He didn't hold back his theories, and tried to sell the idea of individuality to her, explaining in every possible way, that in true love, partners encourage each other's progress and not restrict it for selfish reasons.

They talked to each other till three in the morning, after which, her father gave up. It was not that she didn't understand what her father meant, or tried to convey, but in no way would she have him tell her that her love was not true, or was unimportant. She even thought about his words later before she slept, and knew that whatever he said was right. But she was too scared to give up what she had finally found; what she had always wanted–perfect love.

She came back to Mumbai after a week, and talked to Ashish about applying in foreign Universities for her Masters, which saddened him. He went off to a friend's house in anger and disappointment, and stayed there for two days, as a result of which, she finally agreed never to bring up that topic. To make her happy again, and indirectly securing his relationship with Sara, Ashish bought her a big diamond ring, after which, she believed that they were officially engaged.

After a month, she was tired of him simply lying around in the house. She decided and finally persuaded him to join his family business. She also thought that work would keep him away from his friends: which turned out to be true, but what she didn't realize was that it applied to her too. After he started working with his father, she realized that his father was a very strict man, apart from being a very extravagant provider. She talked to Ashish about taking up a job herself, to which he reacted rather harshly and gave her strict instructions to never think about it, not realizing that she wasn't talking about earning money, but utilizing her time. As a result, she picked up her reading glasses and resumed her interest in reading.

She read the books in the following order: *Lady Chatterly's Lover, Atlas Shrugged, Moth Smoke, Guns, Germs, and Steel, Equus, The Globalization Reader, Lord of the Flies, Another Week on the Concord and Merrimack Rivers, Women Who Run with the Wolves, Surely You're Joking, Mr. Feynman!, Barbarians at the Gate, Requiem for a Dream, Counterculture Through the Ages, The Tao of Physics* and *Wuthering Heights.* Sara was reading fifteen to sixteen hours a day, and never bothered Ashish when he came home after work. Except every Sunday, she hardly read at all, and they spent the entire day together.

But this Sunday was different from the others, and as she moved to the kitchen, wearing her shorts and tee, she reminded Ashish who was sound asleep in the bed, "You remember our plan for today?"

She heard no reply, and therefore tried again, "Ashish, we have to go to the mall right now. Get up."

"Right now?" Ashish groaned.

"Yes, It's already nine. And the author will be there by eleven. Please wake up now," she said.

"Can't we go in the evening?" His voice cleared, which suggested that he had pulled his head out of the blanket.

"No. Right now means right now. And you promised!

Don't forget. Get your ass out of the bed now," she commanded.

They reached the mall at half past eleven in the morning. On their way to the bookstore, Ashish asked, "So, what's the book's name?"

"*The Memoirs of awakening*," Sara replied.

"Is that some spiritual shit?"

"Maybe. I have read his first book. It was amazing. This second book is getting even more interesting reviews."

"What's the author's name?" he asked.

"Ayan."

"Ayan what?"

"I don't know. Ask him when you meet him."

"Oh, I am not talking to him. I am not going inside the book store." he said, taking out his cell phone, "I have to make some calls. I will be there in a while." And he walked away while Sara entered the book-store. She browsed through some books that were kept on the giant platform. It displayed books that dealt with words such as 'demand', 'recently released', and 'best-sellers'. She hadn't read any of those books, and got a sick feeling about not having read much. She had that feeling whenever she was inside a book-store, and it was based on the assumption that every book is worth reading, and the unending shelves of books around her made her feel like an insignificant entity amidst the knowledgeable.

She spotted the author almost suddenly, but didn't care to walk around like other people who were present for the same purpose. She picked up his novel from the shelf and started to flip through it, while the author was giving a little talk about how he came to write this book, what was his inspiration, and how thankful he was to his faithful readers. After the talk was over, and the little crowd gently seemed to make way for her, she stood up and walked to him smiling with his book in her hand. He wore a black tee, black sunglasses and had a beard. "Hi." she said.

He looked up at her and froze. Because he was wearing sunglasses, his sudden reaction gained a favorable chance of being ignored and not misunderstood as rude behavior. He put out his hand for the book that she held. She handed it to him quickly. He took his pen and opened the first page of the book, when she spoke "I loved your first book. It was marvelous." And she went quiet.

He didn't know what to write, and she noticed that his hand which held the pen was shaking.

"Hey, Sara," came the voice of Ashish from a distance.

"Yeah," she said looking back, "I am getting the novel signed."

Ashish came up "Come baby, let's go." Ashish had nowhere to go, and he had no intentions earlier of even stepping inside the book-store, but after noticing that the author was so young, and considering that Sara was so fond of his writing, he made a point of jumping in between them, and adding that additional 'baby', to announce, or brag about, his possession of her.

Ayan noticed his presence, and his hands stopped

shaking. He exhaled deeply, and wrote:

> I am only breathing as I have no words left to say. Your presence has made me forget that there is a language.

He closed the book, and handed it back to Sara. She smiled and left with Ashish.

Chapter - 16

04 July, 2009

Dearest,

It's the Fourth of July, and I saw you today. It is the reason why I am withholding my breath and very reluctantly releasing it, somehow preventing an outburst of tears. I can't close my eyes, as I picture you in my mind.

I have cried after a very long time, and once again because of you. How is it, that after achieving so much in thought, I have not yet come to defeat you even in the minutest sense?

How is it that your you gradually moved through my subconscious, and I consciously became unresponsive to the greatest take-over in History?

How could I be so foolish and how could love not be wrong?

I saw you smile today. I have never seen you smile before, or maybe I have forgotten, and a thought went across my mind. Maybe someday in the future, I will have my name written on your lips, causing them to widen in happiness. But I care to say now, in this moment, and in the next, and in every moment after that: I love you, and I miss you. I miss you so much, so much that neither these flowing tears, nor the wounded heart that is screaming and yearning for hope, nor my secluded, banished mind, sitting somewhere alone in its defeat, could have possibly anticipated. And therefore now, I close my eyes and let the tears flow from every possible corner as they choose to, defeating, subjugating, torturing, and leaving me with the absolute realization of my countless weaknesses.

15 July, 2009

Dearest,

I close my eyes, again and again, as I get haunted by your hollow beauty penetrating through the most dark, undisclosed chambers of my mind. What are

your secrets? I secretly wish to unravel them and claim you to be mine. I am the blood in your veins; when will you see this?
Perhaps you need to bleed first. Perhaps you need to drown and understand the meaning of life as opposed to the perceptions stored in your feeble mind. Perhaps you need to be more awake for illusions to haunt you, so you can experience your darkest nightmares whilst you are still living. Perhaps you need to wash away that smell as it stinks of an influence. Perhaps you need to die, not in reality, but in my mind. This is too morbid a thought whereas I am too peaceful a man.
I am tired, full of hatred, still fanatically endeavoring and craving for the hour of our union. I hope you are smiling, for that brings tears into my eyes, like music playing in the ears of a prisoner, reminding him of the deadliest truth: hope. Before I stop to breathe and leave this land, I would like to see you, even if I have lost my eyes, to once again experience your presence around me.

24 July, 2009

Dearest,
There was only one thing missing from the promulgation of this truth: Music. After listening to this beautiful track, although for reasons vastly different from the ones tonight, I submit myself to

sinking into your thoughts and only yours. Angel, I have not the faintest idea where to begin, or what I should write! Should I write a story to bewilder you, to surprise you, maybe to be able to make you cry and realize my intentions? Or should I indulge in poetry, toil through day and night producing new thoughts, or paradoxes and juxtapositions of crimes of nature and compare your love with them? Am I selfish? Am I rightfully yours to begin with? Or the right question should be: Are you rightfully mine? The answer hovers in the darkness for a while after which it runs out of breath and dies. I am in no state of making amendments except for pushing some air inside my lungs every time your thought tries to withdraw life from my body.

15 August, 2009

My love,

I feel like I am searching for a stone with a message engraved on it, hoping to believe that there is a meaning, desperately wanting to find sense, anxiously perspiring with sweat on my forehead, waiting, just waiting for a plan, waiting to be guided, waiting to be rescued from these chains of harsh times. I am on my knees, begging to be crowned with the knowledge to understand a simple solution to this torment. It seems as if insanity will take me over in any moment.

But I have learned to be silently holy. I have learned that a very lively part inside of me is dead, which is why I am quieter than quiet nowadays. Tears do not flow like they used to anymore. In fact, they too have abandoned me. My chest is heavy at all times, and it directly links up with my breathing. That is sorrow. I know it, because I have come to live with it for a very long time. I have never confronted it, except when you have unconsciously dared me to. I am a weak person, because I can't stand the thought of loneliness anymore, but I can't abandon it after having gladly proposed it to be my willful companion for life.

I often see myself standing in the midst of a storm with my hands open, in my dreams. I can't see the face but I know it's me. And in that apocalyptic wasteland, withered and sabotaged, by storms and rains and earthquakes, in that vehemently dense wind, I see my body dissolve into nothingness.

Last night, I dreamed about my father. He was walking towards a stream of water, probably a rivulet. I called for him repeatedly, asking him to stop. But he kept walking. I ran back to get some help, but nobody cared. And when I got back, all I could see was his head which was sinking into the water, as if he were still walking inside the water body, in full acknowledgement and acceptance,

of his death. I was helpless and roamed about the stream with no sign of any human existence.
Was it a sign, that I hold myself responsible for my father's death? I have been pondering this since.

Ayan had written around two hundred letters by now. But in this fervent approach, he had forgotten to perform any of the much needed chores. The only food he consumed was one cigarette after another, and occasionally, some chocolates, biscuits, and tea. He had locked himself up in the room and was completely devoid of any contact with the outside world as he had stopped using a phone, and the messages that did make it through those bolted doors were the ones in the form of mails.

Whenever he woke up, he had a sudden blackening of his vision and experienced an effect of fainting. He would sit down on the bed or the chair or the couch, whichever was near, and wait till he regained the clarity of his vision. He knew it happened because of the weakness, but after a time, he was used to it and didn't care at all. As days passed, he ate less, played more music, and wrote letters.

13 September, 2009

Dearest,
I have lost this battle, like every other. I simply want to lie down and close my eyes, I want to take off my clothes, and float on a river like a log of

wood. I want to be buried inside the earth, so I can hear in every moment, the world walking over me, trampling my presence with their unconscious contempt. I want to be as strong as truth, which has no emotions and defines both the nature of good and bad.

What have I achieved? What have I known? After knowing so much, if I have lost everything, then I have known nothing.

I think about the grass that grows on the land, I have a great respect for the land. I respect its wisdom, when compared to mine. I don't like the trees much, because I don't find them beautiful, except for the one growing outside in the garden.

I remember when I looked into a river for the first time in my life, I was unable to produce any thought, and that irritated me very much. I know nature has a captivating beauty of its own, but it has no truth save what you see. And I don't have enough time to stare into meaningless, thought-obstructing creations meant to inspire humans. Nature reminds a man of his home, not the house he has lived in his entire life, but his true home. There is no truth beyond that for a human being to experience–finding a natural source that judges him without having the characteristics to question.

14 October, 2009

Love,
You can always picture me sitting inside a dark room, on a chair, with my hands firmly placed on the keyboard and my fingers punching its keys, my ears rejoicing with the music, the sound of every single note when an alphabet comes to life while constantly being judged by my eyes.

I have little hope that I might sleep now. It's my third day without sleep, and I have developed a severe pain at the back of my head. I wish I could sleep, so maybe in my dreams I might meet you again, and maybe this time, words would appear in the shape of sounds and enchant your senses. I have no dreams except to see you again, and see you again and again. I wonder sometimes: if I ever meet you, with the sole purpose of having a conversation, how badly would I perform?

Would I fumble and prove to be an unworthy lover?

Would I beg and demand, proving myself to be uncultured and insane?

Or would I be quieter than quiet again, proving that this world is not a place for us. For you belong in heaven, and without you I may suffer for the rest of my life, knowing that I made a mistake of falling in love with an angel.

27 November, 2009

Dearest,

I have only just woken up, and you are all that is in my mind. To breathe in the illusion of liberty seems like an uncultivated reality. Hopelessness is the reward of sleeping without having anything to dream about, and simplicity a virtue when reality seems to be controlled by someone else.

What truth shall I seek, O' dearest of strangers.

If I could, I would walk every step of these thousand miles that separate us, and hold you in my arms.

If I could, I would fill your heart with the songs of my love, deluging it, in the attempt that nothing, not even the beauty of Eden could replace it.

If I could, I would lay down every known and unknown happiness man has ever explored, down at your feet.

If I could, I would build us a beautiful house with my own hands, and write our names on every brick that will form its walls.

If I could, I would spend each second of my life taking care of you, loving you, and staying beside you.

If I could, I would take long walks with you alongside a creek, and kiss you at every chance

I get.

If I could, I would read poetry from your eyes, every time you look at me with the contentment of having found true love.

If I could, I would have your name embedded in my heart, so that when my corpse putrefies, the only graceful thing remnant is you.

If I could, I would steal life from the hands of God, for you are the only reason I want to stay alive in the next moment, and for eternity.

Meanwhile, I walk aimlessly, neglecting everything potentially essential—throwing away my goals, my true reason to survive, pretending to have understood the fate of goodness, the very lesson of honor, the very songs of dignity, and the sounds of speech that men love the most—of lies.

Ayan kept the pen down, stood up, and had walked only a few steps before he fainted.

Chapter - 17

Ayan woke up after a long slumber, but the headache not only stopped him from functioning properly but restrained him in the bed. His eyes opened, and he noticed Mezz sitting on the chair, reading letters from the notebook.

"Hey," Ayan grumbled.

"Hey, tea?" Mezz asked, and walked to the kitchen before waiting for his answer.

"When did you come?"

"Last night." Mezz replied from the kitchen. "It's Sunday today. I am leaving for London in a few days. I told you about that course, didn't I? Anyway, when I came here in the evening, you were sleeping. I thought you were dead and that maybe I am now involved in a potential crime scene. I mean, who knows, I could be held as a f...ing suspect now. But then you weren't dead, so I put you up on the bed and slept on the couch! You've started drinking too?"

"Oh no," said Ayan, "I have stopped eating. It's because of weakness."

"Then why don't you eat, you dumbass? Are you working on a new book? And what's with the pile of letters? Setting a world record?" He shouted from the Kitchen.

"I saw her in Mumbai," Ayan replied. "I went there for the book release. She was there, in the book-store to see me."

"To see you?" Mezz asked in surprise. "And?"

"And nothing. It was like an ambush. I was nonplussed."

"Hmm! I understand," he said. "I read your second novel. It was really brilliant." He entered the room holding a steel glass filled with tea for Ayan.

"Thanks," Ayan said, taking the glass from his hand.

"I have read it has become a best-seller, is it true?"

"I have no clue," Ayan answered.

"You don't talk to your publishers?"

"My phone is off."

"Since when?"

"It's been," Ayan said thoughtfully, "around six months, I guess."

"What about e-mail? Facebook?" Mezz asked, surprised.

"They cut my internet off because I haven't paid my bills."

"And what's with the Jesus Christ look?"

"It's not a Jesus Christ look, it's my Rabindra Nath Tagore look."

"He had a bigger beard," Mezz said.

"I will reach there one day," Ayan said, as he picked up his guitar, and started playing it.

"You've lost weight. Lot of weight. I am worried about you, man. I mean, you're a writer, not a rockstar. You are supposed to be acting like a sensible person, and not locking yourself up in a room and taking drugs."

"I am not taking drugs," Ayan replied calmly.

"Well, you look like a drug addict."

"I am not taking drugs," Ayan said, looking into his eyes.

"What have you been doing then?"

"Composing music. Writing letters. Reading. What about you?"

"I just got out of a relationship," Mezz replied.

"You?"

"Yeah, it was getting serious."

"Tell me about the girl," Ayan said.

"She is a lecturer. Intellectual Property Rights. And she is middle-aged, not old." Mezz paused.

"Do you think it's time I met Sara?" Ayan asked, still playing his guitar.

"I don't know," Mezz said thoughtfully, "but if there is a right time, then this is as good as any."

Ayan nodded. "You know what; I have decided to write my third book now."

"Great!"

"I think it's going to be a play, or maybe a short story, or might be a novel. It's going to be about a womanizer, something related to his multiple personalities. I can give him disorders." At this point, he was talking to himself.

"Go take a bath and shave off the beard. We're going out."

Ayan stood and looked out of the the window, "Come here, and look at the tree."

Mezz glanced at the tree, "Wow, it's grown considerably."

Ayan smiled, "Beautiful, isn't it?"

"Yeah, it is something."

At night, Ayan prepared himself to write his third book. He took a shower, shaved off his beard, clipped his nails, tied up his long hair, and once again looked presentable. He sat on the chair and placed his fingers on the keyboard of his computer, but didn't type anything for a very long time. He then retreated to the couch, holding a pencil and a few sheets of paper, and started making notes on the story, after which he fell asleep.

He woke up the next morning, and looked less presentable than he did the previous night. He took a long shower pondering about the story, and then about Sara. He was stuck with the idea of meeting her. It could be that he lacked the courage to turn it into action, or the simple assurance achieved by the time he had spent without chasing her might have convinced him that there was no need to meet her any more. He came out of the bathroom and looked at the time: it was afternoon, a cold reminder that he hadn't eaten anything yet. He sat in front of the computer and started typing his story. After typing a paragraph, he erased it. He wrote another paragraph and erased it too. He wrote and erased seven more times. He did so because after writing, he would compare the text to his previous works. Tired of not getting anywhere, he slept.

He grew weaker as the weeks passed, and his appetite was reduced to a couple of eggs, a glass of milk, excessive amount of tea and cigarettes, a packet of biscuits, and Pizzas that he ordered once or twice a month. His eyes would hurt easily, preventing him from reading continuously for hours. After a while, his joints started to hurt too, perhaps due to lack of physical exercise. He decided to start working out, but never did, because of the weakness leading to laziness.

He read about many religions, and concluded from them that man's supreme duty is to labour. He decided that he won't waste any more of his time, but was soon down with fever, and therefore, rested more. During the span of time in which he couldn't move out of the bed, he wrote an essay titled *"The concept of Right and Wrong."* He also read Machiavelli's *Discourses*, and then Karl Marx's *Dialectical Materialism*, and after that, Kant's *Critique of Pure Reason*.

After recovering from the fever he started working on his book, but after a few days, he fell sick again, and this routine continued.

He completed his book and submitted it to his publishers in one and a half years, in May, 2011. After meeting them, he also came to know that both of his previous books had become national best-sellers now, and his second book was even selling internationally. In the same year, he was approached by several newspapers asking him to write articles for them on any subject he chose. Ayan accepted without asking the price they were offering for the service.

The first article he wrote was about how an individual starts his life in nothingness, and during half his life, toils his way upwards in the corporeal world, craving to achieve almost every joy made for man by man, and then later, in his old age, retires from the same joys he had earned, believing that it was all an illusory good, and that peace is in detachment. It was titled: *Poverty is a state of Nirvana.*

He was greatly lashed by Economists but appreciated by his fans, who he believed didn't understand a word. He received an email from Mezz saying, "I read your article. I have got a job in Pune. Brilliant one. Will be making a lot of money. Screw you."

He smiled, wondering when people would understand humour, and played Bach's Air on the G string, on his computer. In a moment, he collapsed and fell from the chair. Ayan opened his eyes and witnessed everything blurred around him, and a sudden pain in his head caused him to close them again, and he was unconscious. The second time he opened his eyes, there was light in the room, and he could feel that he wasn't wearing his usual clothes, but something else entirely, something which he hadn't worn ever. His eyes were busy familiarizing his mind with the room, which oddly looked like a hospital room. He felt the sudden pang of pain in his forehead, which made him touch it, and it finally made him acquainted with the bandage that was wrapped around it. Now, he had confirmed that it was a hospital room; therefore he closed his eyes and was unconscious again. The third time he opened his eyes, he saw a person wearing a white coat standing on his right. He murmured, "What's the date today?"

The man informed him about the time and date, and said, "Take rest."

Ayan obeyed him like a child and fell asleep.

Chapter - 18

"Good morning, Mr Ayan," the doctor said, "How are you doing?"

Ayan was sitting on the edge of the bed, his toes touching the floor. "What happened to me, Doctor?"

"You fainted in your house and bruised your head," the doctor replied. He was a middle aged man, wearing a blue shirt and a long white coat.

"And who brought me here?" Ayan asked.

"You don't remember? You called your uncle and told him to take you to a hospital."

"I don't remember," he whispered looking down at the

floor. "How long have I been here?"

"Four days." The Doctor paused, "It was not only the injury, you had very high fever too. In fact, you were given a blood transfusion. Anyway, I need to ask you a few questions."

"Sure," Ayan said, looking at him.

"Have you been sick lately?" The doctor asked calmly.

"A lot. Yes." Ayan replied.

"A lot? Care to share?"

"Fevers, on and off. Physical weakness, common cold."

"Did you see a Physician?" he asked.

"No."

"Then how did the fever go?"

"I used to take pills for fever and the cold from a chemist. And they worked. But then it often came back again." Ayan paused, "I know the problem, I wasn't eating anything. I didn't take care of my body and I guess I lost immunity."

After listening to him quietly, the doctor asked, "And for how long have you been experiencing the coming and going of these problems?"

"About a year," Ayan replied, thoughtfully.

The doctor was amazed and irritated at the same time, but kept such reactions from showing on his face. He asked seriously: "You never thought it could be something serious?"

Ayan sensed that the doctor was displeased by his answer. "I am sorry. Have you found something serious?" he asked politely.

"I can't say anything right now, Ayan. But that is the reason why I am asking you about your condition before you were hospitalized. We do have your medical history from your uncle, but since you have been living alone for a long time, I have to know from you. Is there anything else than the fever? Any kind of pain in your body parts? Anything unusual that troubled you?"

"Well, I feel pain in every part of my body, especially in the joints. And as I have told you, there is weakness all the time." Ayan thought and said: "Stuff like that only."

The doctor suddenly remembered something and asked, "Also, have you ever fainted before?"

"Yes," Ayan said, "around seven times. And yes, I also had the blackening of my vision a lot. Blackouts, it's called?"

"Seven times?" The doctor was stunned, "Why didn't you consult a doctor if you had so many problems?"

"I thought it was because of weakness, as I wasn't..."

"You thought?" The doctor interrupted. "That's a wrong way to think. I don't get it. That is very irresponsible." The doctor sighed, told Ayan to rest, and left.

Within a week, Ayan was sitting on the hospital bed, and his uncle on the chair next to it, expecting to be told that it was some minor health problem caused by his extremely careless attitude. He thought he would pretend to listen to the doctor's ramblings; and maybe even consider if there was a good piece of advice somewhere, but all he wanted at this moment was fresh air and a cigarette. On the other hand, his uncle looked very serious and afraid, waiting for what the doctor had to say about Ayan. The doctor was standing in front of them, talking to a nurse in what was medical terminology, but gibberish to the two sitting in front of him. The nurse left.

"Mr Ashok, we have Ayan's final reports," the doctor said. "He has been diagnosed with cancer in his blood cells."

Both of them went into a state of shock, and then, silence. The doctor waited, allowing them to have a minute to understand the situation.

"Is there a treatment for that?" Ayan asked.

"Of course there is, Ayan. There is no such thing as a guaranteed treatment or cure, and I won't lie to you. But yes, many patients suffering from this type of cancer have been treated."

"How bad is my case?"

"It is bad," the doctor said.

"I don't understand. I have had it for a year and I was alright?" Ayan said, trailing the genesis of the downfall of his health. "What you have is a chronic form of Leukemia, but because of no treatment at all, it has worsened into a very aggressive state. It is very serious at this stage, so we'll have to start your treatment right away. And you have had it for more than a year."

A long silence followed.

"What is the treatment, doctor?" His uncle spoke for the first time, in a weakened voice.

"Mr Ashok, you must have heard of Chemotherapy. We'll also put him in the waiting list for a bone-marrow transplant." Silence reigned again. After a minute, the doctor looked at Ayan and asked politely, "Any more questions?"

"What are the chances? And please give me the truth, doctor." Ayan asked.

"Ayan, it's not completely mathematics. We see miracles everyday here," he said sympathetically. "You will have to have faith. Do you believe in God?"

"Not the one who falls within your definition of God, no!"

The doctor smiled at the answer but was unsure of what to make of it. Ayan's uncle spoke, "If there is something, you can tell us." His voice was cracking, which was a sign that he was worried sick.

"I am not concealing anything from you," the doctor said. "In fact, I want you to accompany me to my office. I will explain everything to you." He looked at Ayan and said, "You rest now."

And they left the room. Ayan knew that it was very serious despite the doctor's assurances. His uncle stayed inside the doctor's office for almost half an hour. Ayan believed that his uncle must have broken down, which is why, he didn't come to meet him directly after that, but after an hour.

Ayan was discharged after a week, but his treatment continued, and certain dates had been assigned on which he was supposed to visit the hospital. He settled in his uncle's home, and most of the things were brought there from his apartment. He rested most of the time. In the first week, he witnessed sorrow on the faces of people who came to meet him in his room, especially his family members, whom he didn't care much about, except his uncle. After a week, that look on their faces changed to a pitying mask they had to wear whenever they stepped inside the room. They all sat with him, genuinely caring about him.

Finally, one day, after he woke from a long slumber, he found Mezz sitting on the chair next to his bed, eating an apple from the basket of fresh fruits that somebody must have brought. He was wearing a black suit, white shirt, a black tie, and polished shoes.

"They tell you to dress up like James bond?" Ayan murmured.

"What the hell happened to you?" Mezz uttered after listening to Ayan's voice.

"Who told you?" Ayan asked, getting up and adjusting his back against the pillow.

"Are you kidding me? It's in every newspaper." Mezz sniggered at Ayan's confused look. "My dad told me."

"And who told your dad?" Ayan asked.

"Everyone knows. It's cancer, right? Is it serious or treatable? You look awful."

"Well, being ugly is a beautiful thing," Ayan said. "People do not remember you for your face but for who you are." He smiled. "It's good to see you. How is work?"

"Work is? Work was," he said. "I said that my friend is dying, so I need a month off. They didn't understand. So f… you, I said and resigned. So tell me, how serious is it?"

"I am okay. They are trying, even though it's pretty bad, as you can see."

Mezz looked around the room and then at Ayan's weakened condition with an expression Ayan had never seen before. It was one of extreme seriousness, the kind in which one doesn't appreciate any humour, in which silence is the best companion, in which words often open the gates for tears.

"I came here as fast as I could. This can't be happening." Mezz said.

He had tears in his eyes. "You're my brother. What the f…, man!" he said, and tears started flowing. He didn't move, didn't weep, didn't sob, didn't say anything, as if practicing immense control.

"I am sorry," he said, wiping off his tears. "This won't happen again," he said and smiled.

Ayan had never seen him cry before, except when they were kids and everytime something was taken away from Mezz, he would cry. But as they grew up, he banished tears a long time ago and a lot faster than children his age did.

"What was that?" Ayan asked calmly.

"Nothing," Mezz said, and Ayan noticed the same pitiful mask on his face too.

"I have been thinking, and I wanted to meet you especially for this," Ayan said.

"For what?"

"I want you to find Sara."

Mezz sighed. "I don't understand."

"I want you to find out where she is. What she is doing right now! I want to know who she is, what she likes, what she dislikes," Ayan emphasized. "I have spent all this time loving an idea of that girl. The truth is, I don't even know who she is. I don't even remember her voice any more, Mezz. What am I loving here? What have I loved? A ghost with a mask?"

"And after you have found your answers?" Mezz asked, "What if she is quite pleasant? Or appalling? What are your intentions?"

"I can't go to Mumbai," Ayan said, "I don't know about the future. It hangs between I may and I may not. I know I should have done this a long time ago." He paused. "I never should have waited, but I hope you understand that I am not talking about confrontation or confession right now; it's acknowledgement."

"So, you want her to know about you?" Mezz asked.

"I do, but I can't find an appropriate way of doing it–a quiet, silent way for a perfectly executed disclosure." Ayan said. "It's hard to live with the fact that my life could come to an end, and she wouldn't even know that I loved her; that somewhere in this world, I loved her with all my heart." He looked at Mezz.

"Look, we can't do this alone," Mezz said, after thinking for a while, "We'll have to contact some sort of private detective agency for this type of work. I know this because Lawyers often require the services of Private Investigators."

"Do you know any?" Ayan asked.

"As a matter of fact, I do. Think about all the questions you have and write them down. Every detail you might want to know. Obviously I can't bring him here, but I'll get you all the information."

"You can bring him here," Ayan said, "Just make sure no one from the family gets to know. All they need is someone to stick around me so I am entertained, and I guess your presence would save them from this duty."

"You've got a television here," Mezz said, pointing at it.

"Oh yeah, it looks beautiful, doesn't it?" Ayan smiled.

Chapter - 19

Now had come the period of silence. He refused to read the newspaper, as the world didn't interest him anymore. He had a pile of selected books kept on his left side, whose presence he thoroughly enjoyed while gaining a sort of special strength from them. He often scribbled on his notepad, but told Mezz that it wasn't anything worth publishing; he was determined to destroy these writings if his condition ever was to become fatal.

Mezz visited him at every opportunity he could get, but of course, that was managed in accordance with Ayan's condition. With the passing of each day, Ayan's face grew paler and he grew thinner. He had also started to experience several rather expected side-effects of the treatment, which took a large chunk of his intellectual responsiveness and converted it into dullness and lethargy, and robbed him of the general aura that surrounded him once. But whenever they did meet, they made fun of politics, films, writers, and famous people, and anything they could lay their hands on.

After a week, Mezz came to visit Ayan with an old man, a gawky figure, wearing a suit that did not fit his body, which made Ayan especially skeptical about his role, as he was the man appointed by Mezz to find Sara. The man shook hands with Ayan but did not say a word. He was certainly a lonely man, Ayan thought, judging from his dressing sense, which only meant that he either did not care about how he looked, or had no one who cared about how he looked.

"This is Mr Dev," Mezz said, rubbing his eyes.. "He has brought all the information you wanted to know about Sara." He yawned and simultaneously opened the file, which was in his hand. "So, you want me to read it to you right now, or would you like to read it yourself?"

"You read," Ayan said.

"Okay!" he said, counting the pages and looking at the pictures with not much seriousness. "Name, address, what the f…," Mezz cried, surprised and looked at the old man. "She is married?" He turned to Ayan, and both exchanged a look of shock.

"Everything is in the file," Mr Dev said in his hoarse voice.

"Are you kidding me? This can't be true," Mezz said,

shuffling through the pages and checking the pictures again. "Okay, it is her." He looked at Ayan and said, "She is married."

After a moment of silence, during which Mezz continued his own silent investigation, he spoke, "She's married to a Mr Ashish; here, take a look at these pictures."

Mezz gave Ayan the picures, while concentrating on the text.

"This is complicated stuff." Mezz murmured.

"For how long has she been married?" Ayan asked, after looking at the pictures.

"One and a half years. The marriage isn't going well. In fact, they are on the verge of separation," Mezz said.

"What? How?" Ayan asked.

"Wait, I am reading how she got married. It's too messy," Mezz said.

"It's given how she got married?" Ayan said with a confused expression.

"It's not what you think; it's not that simple," Mezz said, his eyes glued to the text. Ayan waited impatiently.

"Apparently, she got pregnant, according to this report, and married that guy in haste, also secretly. She didn't tell her parents, which is why her parents have abandoned her. How can so much of non-stop shit happen in a person's life?" He cried, looking at Ayan.

"What do you mean?" Ayan asked.

"I think it's bullshit; made-up," he said, indirectly attacking the old man, who was listening to everything quietly.

"Mezz," Ayan said, "behave!" He paused, "What else is in

it?" He asked, noticing that Mr Dev had no reaction.

Mezz opened the file again. "Well, there is this– there is no baby, which means she must have had an abortion. Let me read this whole part," Mezz said and another long silence followed.

"According to the story, she got married, and he started working with his father in their family business. After three months of their marriage, he went to the U.S. for two weeks, to China for a week, and continued travelling to many different places without her, for business purposes. He had also prohibited her to work or study further. Do you know which subject she has done her graduation in?" He paused, looking at Ayan, "History."

Ayan smiled. He genuinely felt happy for a moment.

"Anyway she left him. The reason could be that she found out that he was cheating on her as he now lives in that same apartment with another woman." He paused, "Of course, he was cheating on her."

He continued again, "She's living at blahblah, address in Mumbai, alone. She also has a job as a primary school teacher, and that is the only source of her earning," he paused. "Okay! Her life sucks badly."

"What about the divorce?" Ayan asked.

"Wait, let me see," Mezz said, and he started looking in the papers. "It's unclear. Can I ask you a question?" Mezz asked Mr Dev, and he nodded a response.

"All this information," Mezz said, "you have provided to us. There's so much of it that we didn't even ask you to find.

I am not complaining, only asking."

"It's not my first case," he replied. "Such information is usually of foremost importance to my clients. The truth is, I am not aware of what the original intentions of the clients are. Even though I always have an idea, but I can never be fully sure. If I hadn't collected this information, you would have sent me again to get it for you, ending up paying me twice the money. You are kids, and I don't exploit kids, sir." Ayan knew that his last remark was directed at Mezz.

"Well, that satisfies me," Ayan said. "I don't understand one thing why would he leave her so soon after the marriage? I mean, betray her."

"They were already living together before they got married. I told you that," Mezz said.

"No, you didn't."

"Oh, I must have missed it," Mezz said, still reading the report, "they were living together for a year."

"It's pretty obvious—the guy is an asshole, not a smart one, but a greedy one. Rich. Loser. He must have wooed Sara in college. Reason could be money. She is pretty and tall and hot and all of the things losers really crave for. He must be convinced that he loves her. Then he started working with his father, saw the benefits of money and got himself in that position where everything comes easy. In this scenario, the basic assumption is that she is fucking dumb. She started to live with him, and then he knocked her up."

"It's too simple." Ayan said. "Life is full of complications, but the roots of truth are always basic and simple." He contradicted himself, giving away how confused he would get in her case.

Mezz said, "I mean, what's with not letting her study further! It's plain chauvinistic, and this makes him a dominating character."

"Mr Dev," Ayan asked, "is there any way you can find out if they are seeking a divorce?"

"But why?" Mezz asked.

"I want to know," Ayan answered.

"What are you thinking?"

Ayan ignored Mezz and turned to Mr Dev, "How far can you extend your services?"

"Depends upon the legal and illegal," the old man answered.

"I don't know about that," Ayan said, "but what if the intentions are to help someone?"

"It still hangs between legal and illegal, sir," he replied.

"You want him to deliver the letters?" Mezz asked in confusion.

"No," he said and turning back to Mr Dev, said, "I still require your services. Even though the information you have provided satisfies every question in our minds, I need you to find more. I want you to find if there is a possibility of a divorce happening in the near future, or has it already been filed? I want you to find out about her financial condition; her relationship with her parents and if it can be fixed?"

"Tell me your plans. What are you thinking?" Mezz interrupted.

"I want to help her," Ayan said.

"Then I will go to Mumbai with him too," Mezz said.

"Yes, I was just going to say that," Ayan said. "Analyze the situation and take action if necessary." He paused, "tell me something, can you help her get a decent job? Or could you, Mr Dev?"

"I am sorry, sir." Mr. Dev answered, professionally.

Mezz, who was rubbing his forehead with his fingers said, "I can help. I know a guy who can get her a good job. A good business job."

"What kind?" Ayan asked.

"He'll make a new kind."

"What would he want?" Ayan asked.

"He's a greedy bastard."

"How much would it take?"

"If we are looking for something permanent, with a guarantee that she won't be dropped off, I guess, around a hundred thousand."

"I want your guarantee, Mezz," Ayan said.

"Well, I would see to it that his word becomes my word. That I can promise and you can trust me," Mezz said.

"Okay, then make it happen as soon as you can. Don't let her find out that she got this job because of someone," Ayan said.

"Don't worry about that. Leave it to me," Mezz said.

"And Mr Dev, I don't know for how long I might need your services. It could be a week, or a month, but I will take care of all the payments as well as your fees."

Mr Dev stood up, shook hands with both of them, and left.

"This is shocking, right?" Mezz said. "I want to ask you something, you're not holding yourself responsible for her situation, are you?"

"Look at my condition; she would have been worse off if she were with me," Ayan said. "I know what you are thinking, but I am not thinking anymore." He paused. "I am not doing anything to prove something to myself or to anybody. Try to think like this: if something happened to you, wouldn't I help you in every possible way? She is the love of my life, and just because I don't know her, doesn't make her a stranger." He paused. "And you too, remember this; she's not a stranger."

Mezz left for Mumbai in two days with Mr Dev, and Ayan was left alone to think about nothing but Sara. Ayan didn't call Mezz on his phone even once while he was in Mumbai, and patiently waited for him to return, almost as if he didn't expect anything anymore. He often wondered about the lemon tree and wished if he could see it once more.

He spent most of the time sleeping, trying to write short stories or listening to music. Finally, after two weeks, his uncle informed him that he had received a call from Mezz, and he was returning to Delhi.

Chapter - 20

Mezz entered the room with Mr Dev. "My King, why is it so dark?" he cried.

"Morning, sunshine" Ayan said, adjusting himself in the bed, "Good morning Mr Dev, how are you?"

Mr Dev simply nodded, while Mezz opened the drapes and the room was filled with light again.

"So, how was the trip?" Ayan asked.

"There is a lot to tell you. A lot." Mezz emphasized. "The divorce has been filed, and the husband has the upper hand. I don't know if she is dumb, or not at all greedy, but I don't think she'd be asking for a lot in the divorce settlement."

"Okay; how is her financial condition?" Ayan asked.

"Her financial condition is shit. Also, she is not in touch with her parents. And there is a friend involved, who is currently helping her financially with almost everything."

"You mean, it's like a debt?"

"Yep, she is living on her own. She has no job. How do you think she is paying the enormous rent? food? Living and all of that?" Mezz explained.

"Tell me about the debt? Do you know who that friend is?" Ayan asked.

"It's a friend of hers from school. She's the only friend she has. So it makes it less of a debt and more of a favor, but when you look at the amount, it kind of makes it a debt again."

"How much is it?"

"We don't have an exact number, as there has been no accounting carried out between the two parties, but according to our calculations, it's around two lakhs." Mezz said.

"And I don't trust that friend of hers. I mean, she doesn't look like the kind who is going to help someone beyond a certain point." He paused. "I mean, sure, she is helping her right now, but not for very long."

"What about the job?" Ayan asked.

"Oh yes, that's done," Mezz said.

"You got her a job?"

"Yep, and a good job. She is a very smart girl, as told to me by her employer." Mezz said.

"The guy we paid, right?" Ayan asked. "And what's the job?"

"It's of a student counselor," Mezz said. "And yes, that's the same guy. He had an interview with her to see what kind of a job would fit perfectly. What he told me, after the interview, was that she is very well-read and knowledgeable. So it was easy for him to find her a job."

"How much is she going to earn?" Ayan asked.

"Around Thirty to Thirty five thousand a month. You don't worry about the money; he makes all those fake work experiences, which gets the person a really good salary. He has to keep up his reputation, after all," Mezz said.

A brief silence followed, and Mezz continued, "I even drove down to her office to check how she was doing. She seemed to be working quite seriously."

"How can we settle this debt?" Ayan asked.

"We can't, I mean, not directly at least," Mezz said.

"Then think indirectly."

Mezz leaned back in the chair and said, "We can make up a story, like how she..." He paused. "No, that's just stupid."

"It can't be done without disclosing the name of the money-provider," Ayan said. "If she is Sara's friend, she is going to talk about it. We need a false story."

"What about her husband? We could use his name, like he is silently helping her, not wanting to disclose the name." Mezz paused, "But that is stupid. How about her parents?"

"That could work," Ayan said. "She is not in touch with them, so it makes sense that they might want to secretly help her."

"But what if she confronts them regarding this?" Mezz

asked.

"Then we'll have to make her become an ungrateful child," Ayan said. "Why do you think she hasn't had even a single conversation with her parents regarding her marriage, or her financial state? What could be the reasons?"

"Ego." Mezz said, thinking, "Hard-headed behavior. Often deception. A person is most convinced when thoughts are put in his mind, when one is influenced by an external source. Self thought has to go through questioning, and is constantly audited by the mind. But an alien thought has the tendency to blind a person, temporarily of course." He paused, "And then at the later stage, it's guilt."

"True," Ayan said, "it's the guilt. Her parents were against the marriage and now she has been proven wrong. So what's the thing a person does to cope with such realizations?"

"One either confronts them or escapes out of embarrassment." Mezz answered.

"Escapes, right," Ayan said.

"You mean her parents don't know about her divorce?" Mezz said. "Interesting. Actually, that makes perfect sense." He paused, thinking, "We tell Mr Dev to pay her a visit–the friend, not Sara. He hands her all the money, clears the debt, takes some sort of proof that it has been paid, but doesn't reveal the provider's name, as it is the provider's wish. Let her be confused; she will end up accepting someone as her silent backer, maybe her parents. Why do we care?"

"Intriguing," Ayan said. "Okay, let's do this. I hope you don't mind Mr. Dev?" Ayan asked, turning to him.

"Not at all, sir." Mr Dev answered.

"Then it's done," Ayan said. Mr Dev shook hands with both of them, and left.

Ayan looked at Mezz and asked, "When you saw her, how did she look?"

"Sad and alone." Mezz answered. "Change, even for good, can be monotonous sometimes."

"And what about you?" Ayan asked, "Are you seeing someone?"

"At this moment? No," he answered. "Do you still write letters to her?"

"No," Ayan answered, "What sense does it make now?"

"Those letters could be your last words to her," Mezz said.

Ayan smiled, as if he rejoiced at the sound of those words,"When this problem started, at the beginning when I was alone, I wondered, why! You know, like why? And then I questioned God. And then I questioned everything around me—animals, nature, even the inanimate objects, everything. And then I was simply lost in nothingness. I closed my eyes and slept. And when I woke up I did it all over again." He paused.

"People won't show their real faces any more, and there is really no need too. I simply smile and try to be positive about everything. And then finally a time comes when I unknowingly become a part of that nothingness, and stop trying. That is the time called 'wait'. None of it makes any sense now—politics, the bloody struggle, movie-stars, fame, which sitcom I was watching, the beautiful girl who has recently moved next to my house, my favorite hang-out spots..."

His voice started to break, so he paused and held himself.

"You know, Mezz, we always think we know what consciousness is, but our entire life is lived subconsciously, because we simply refuse to be aware of a simple fact: that every coming moment is not just a moment, it's an opportunity to take ourselves a step further. I am conscious now; this is my conscious self right now. I would've done much more, had I been conscious like I am in this moment." Ayan said.

"The rise of a man does not make him great, nor does it grant him an everlasting fame; it's the fall of the man, and the height, and the dramatic intensity of that fall that makes him God-like."

"Napoleon said something like that," Mezz said.

"It's the truth, Mezz. And the truth is forever the same," Ayan said, "I mean, what is immortality when this very planet that we live on has an end? There are numerous philosophies that comfort human minds on immortality, and I do not deny death–it's as certain as my illness, but I do question the painted valley of immortality, and I do not mean those who have become immortal by their works, I mean those who claim to define it. What is this immortality?" He sighed. "It's remembrance. It's as simple as that, and it is directly linked with forgetfulness. You are immortal as long as you are remembered, and you are immortal only in the eyes of those who remember you. And that makes everything immortal for a while—a fucking joke, an incident, a painting without a name on it, an emotion, a confused state, a moment of absolute sense, every fucking thing." He paused to breathe, and continued, "you remain immortal until you are forgotten; you die the very moment no one remembers that you existed."

Mezz kept quiet, unsure of what to say, but he preferred listening to what Ayan was thinking. "I have wanted to talk to you about something related to Sara," Ayan said. "I want to discuss it with you, but I don't want any objections."

"Sure."

"I want you to go to Mumbai and give the money to Sara's friend, not Mr Dev. I can't trust him to convey things properly." Ayan said.

"I understand. I'll do it," Mezz said.

After Ayan explained to him what he had been planning, there was a long silence in the room. Neither of them spoke a word. Ayan wrote a cheque for the money to pay Sara's debt; this was the third cheque he had written by now: the first being for Sara's job; the second for Mr Dev's fees. Mezz left for Mumbai the next day.

On the same day, Ayan's health worsened, and he remained unconscious for a few days, and then, semi-conscious for a few more. Mezz had returned from Mumbai three days before Ayan regained consciousness and was ready to have another meeting. On the first day of the new month, Ayan and Mezz finally had their much anticipated meeting.

Chapter - 21

"Dude, you are growing uglier and uglier," Mezz said.

Ayan chuckled, "I never cared about external beauty. Of course, it's the primary requirement for everybody to indulge in love, and to seek reciprocated love. It's more in demand to be a marketable product than a true lover in today's world. The entire cosmetic industry is running on this simple fact."

Mezz chuckled.

"You won't believe what I dreamed about last night," Ayan said.

"About what?"

"I dreamed of being in a hayfield."

"You mean like from the movie: *Gladiator*?"

"No," Ayan said, laughing, "more like the *Shawshank Redemption* one. I am pretty sure that is where I had the visual from."

"I remember that one," Mezz said thoughtfully.

"Do you ever look into the sky?" he asked after a moment. "It's beautiful, much more beautiful than the face of the person we love, whose beauty has demands, whose personality requires compatibility."

"Since when did you turn into a nature lover?" Mezz asked, surprised.

"No, it's about the love, which is beyond the love between two people. This love doesn't demand anything in return, doesn't expect, doesn't disappoint, doesn't judge. It doesn't care if I am beautiful or ugly, rich or poor, dumb or smart. It's the several forms of purity that are constantly present for you, even though being mere abstractions, they are more alive than the most alive beings in this universe. Do you understand what I am saying?"

"Not a clue," Mezz said. "It seems like you are unknowingly talking about God."

Ayan laughed, "No, I am not talking about God. I am talking about believing in the most beautiful illusions. They are my only options of stealing happiness amidst monotony, pain, and death."

Mezz stayed quiet for a moment, then changed the subject by talking about his trip. "By the way, the work in

Mumbai is done."

"What happened? Tell me everything," Ayan said.

"I went to her place as a private investigator, told her about the situation and the awkward arrangement I was there to make. She hesitated at first but she understood."

"See, that is why I wanted you to go," Ayan said, smiling. "You got any proof?"

"No, we wouldn't need it," Mezz said, "She is not greedy. Had she been a miser, she wouldn't have lent Sara that kind of money in the first place."

"Look, all I need is a confirmation from you," Ayan said, "Thanks, man."

Mezz ignored Ayan's words of gratitude and kept quiet for a while. "Now the question is, how do you plan to tell her about your love?" he asked.

"I will write a letter, explaining everything," Ayan said. "I was wondering when we can start on the work I talked to you about in our previous conversation."

"I'll set it up tomorrow, if you are fine with it."

"Make it as soon as possible."

"Sure," Mezz said, reassuringly.

"This is going to be my last letter," Ayan said thoughtfully. "I wonder what she will understand after reading it. Do you think love can be a captivating thought?"

"Of course it can," Mezz said.

"Is it greater than truth?"

"How could love, being a truth itself, be inferior or superior to any?" Mezz asked, rhetorically, "It combines two different perspectives: one, if you are talking about love as a regular romantic feeling for a girl, then its definition changes with every new person, and in it that case, it's open to criticism. But, and this is our second perspective, if you take love as an independent feeling, in its true, pure form, then there are no comparisons."

Both of them kept quiet for a while, after which Mezz spoke, "Is there something you wanna tell me?"

"No," Ayan said, "I have already written it down."

"How is your writing going?" Mezz asked.

"They are not writings, they are ramblings," Ayan said. "I flushed them down the toilet."

"What?" Mezz reacted, surprised. "I thought you'd be producing the best work of your life right now."

"Mezz," said Ayan, "what is a good man? What is goodness? What is honour? Glory? I don't seem to remember any of it now. I used to be so clear about all of these questions. It's the dullness I have acquired in this room."

"There is a self in every human being," Ayan continued, "that the mind doesn't control. For example, impulsive reactions and actions, unbelievable reactions and actions, there are so many things we do, at so many times, which are completely opposite to our personalities. There is love the mind doesn't control, and logically, the fictional heart doesn't exist. And it makes everything so complicated. There is good and there is evil, Mezz, but can you tell the difference? A person is the embodiment of both good and evil; it's the model on which we are formed. I don't know what I am saying; I am just rambling right now, I think I have lost my mind too."

"What is goodness, Ayan?" Mezz said, "It starts with the acknowledgement that there is evil in the world, and every man has the choice to say no to any sort of moral code and enjoy the riches he has earned. One who believes in being kind to others rather than being a f... prick filled with pride and arrogance just because he has achieved something. One who believes in peace rather than slapping someone who is miserably poor and has jumped in front of his car. One who participates in the betterment of his society. One who is not guided by any selfish motives and expects no rewards when he performs his duty as a citizen and helps as a human being. One who does all of this not because it's the word of God or because of any moral code, but because he knows it's the right action." He paused looking at Ayan "I guess that is what goodness is according to your writings."

"Not in that exact form, but it's true," Ayan said. "In simpler terms, one who has accepted neither hell nor heaven, possessing the power to commit any form of sin without having to face any consequences; one who has made the choice to practice self-control, and does not neutralize his existence between good and evil; on the contrary, steps forward on the path of righteousness, is a hero."

"And what is honour?" Mezz asked, smiling.

"I remember now." Ayan smiled too. "Tell me, what are your future plans?"

Mezz took a long breath, "I haven't actually thought

about it. I will find a job easily, and that is how life is going to be, I suppose."

"And what about your love life? Still don't believe in love?" Ayan asked, interestedly.

"I can't. It doesn't make sense to me." Mezz said, "For example, I don't see an old couple, who have spent their entire lives together and wonder if that is true love. Majority of people in this world choose their partners on sexual grounds. And then later, they adapt. I mean, one marries a person of the same age, or from the same age group. Love doesn't say that the woman I am meant to be with is supposed to fall in my age group. If love is free from the chains of age, race, or any boundaries, then what are the chances that my soul-mate has already spent her life on this planet and is dead! I was simply born a little late."

Ayan was listening to him with a smile. Mezz continued, "There are billions of people in this world, Ayan. And the maximum number of people I am going to meet in my entire life would be around a thousand, including males. So my wife is going to be from those, let's say, six hundred women I am going to meet. Do you see any cosmic universal spark in this eventuality? Only six hundred out of the billions! How can that assure me there isn't a better, or a smarter companion out there than my wife? And that is the reason why people leave each other, couples split, marriages break, and it's not always because of materialistic wealth. This alone proves that love doesn't exist. Human nature is very predictable except for the little things." He sighed, "You tell me, if love is so restricted, then how it can be transcendental? I mean, even your story is ending so bitterly."

"You are not throwing yourself into solitude, are you?" Ayan asked in a worried tone.

Mezz remained quiet, and Ayan continued, "Mezz, I don't regret anything, I swear. I don't regret not having met Sara; yes, I could have, and maybe things would have been different from what they are right now; maybe I wouldn't have been sick too. But do you think, in any scenario, I could have loved her any more than I have?" He looked into Mezz's eyes, "Look, I can't change your mind, but I can give you a thought. A man cannot be happy if he is given exactly what he wishes for, in his definition of a happy life, for we are made this way, intuitively settled to be balanced between the calm and the turbulent. We all need troubles to maintain the sanity in us. It doesn't matter how much I may condemn human nature, but at a time in my life, I will need a woman. I would need her to restore my sanity, to take me out from all my positivity and to bring me closer to impulsiveness, to troubles, to the various thoughts I wouldn't have trodden upon otherwise." He sighed again and continued, "Too much resemblance to a perfect life makes you fall in love with it, and the thought of death not only saddens you but becomes a fear. You need a reason to love death too, Mezz. You need an urge that would make you invite death with open arms; you need a woman." Ayan spoke in Mezz's language, and Mezz, after listening to his words, fell into a deep silence.

After two weeks, Ayan had another dream of a hayfield, except this time he was with Sara. In the dream, they both sat under a tree and talked about the sunset. After he woke up from it, he noted down the entire conversation and every detail from the dream so he may never forget it. He kept it close to him and often had tears in his eyes thinking about her, remembering her image from the dream. On 2nd September, 2011, Ayan's condition worsened and he died.

Chapter - 22

Sara stood in front of the mirror, observing the navy blue long-sleeved shirt and the plain black trousers as she got ready for work. She had been repeating this same routine for quite a few months now–going to work, coming back in the evening, taking a short nap, giving private tuitions to children of different ages, and then finally listening to music and reading.

The day Sara found out that her husband was cheating on her with another woman, she was shattered. She didn't have the strength to leave him; she had never thought that such a moment would come into her life and that too, this soon. The talk they had, which was meant to be a quiet, mature one, turned into a fiasco, and they both hurled abuses, shouted names, provided reasons and examples to present their arguments, and said things that had never been spoken. In one of his arguments, Ashish even confessed that he didn't want to marry this soon and it all happened in confusion, and only after getting married did he realize that he hadn't even lived his life as a bachelor yet. After two hours of useless arguments he left the house banging the door behind him. And that was when she realized that her marriage was over.

The next day, she told Ashish that she loved him and did not want the marriage to be over. They both agreed to start afresh, but thereafter things were not the same. Sara didn't trust him at all, and the lack of trust, blending with the growing suspicions, ruined everything. She finally met her school friend, Trisha, who had shifted to Mumbai with her husband, and told her everything.

It was not surprising when similar events repeated themselves again; with the verbal fights increasing rapidly, the love between them died and their union became a mere agreement. The separation wasn't dramatic as they both decided to leave each other. Trisha had already arranged a small apartment for Sara and paid the rent for six months. Sara didn't ask for any financial support and Ashish didn't offer any. Her salary was only an affirmation of the truth that she had a job. She didn't have the strength to call her parents–such an option never occurred to her. She was too weak and confused and it only became worse after the news that Trisha was moving away to the US with her husband.

During that phase of her life, Sara was completely depressed. She had started to think about killing herself and thoroughly considered the option. She knew one thing—she was completely alone. At that point, she had no idea where her life was going, as she was financially weak, and the guilt of being unable to repay Trisha only strengthened the thought of ending her life.

The only thing that restrained her from taking any drastic, life-threatening step was reading. She was currently reading John Wendell Keller's *Germany, the Wall and Berlin*. Prior to this, she had finished a book on *Cuban Crises*, and was looking forward to reading *The Motorcycle Diaries*. At this point of her life, reading had transformed from a habit into an escape from reality.

After a few days, she received a call from a consultancy asking her to interview for a job opportunity. She was confused at first, mainly because she had never submitted any professional profile to a consultancy, but the desperation overruled all the causes, and she politely noted down the details of the interview, such as the date, address, timings. She was selected in the interview and was offered a much better job in terms of salary. She agreed at once.

At night, she prayed to God and thanked him. She was relieved but not happy; happiness was nowhere in her life, but this recent development at least brought a ray of hope. The next day she joined work, and after a few days, found a satisfactory routine building up as the level of association her job offered, helped her momentarily forget the dilemmas. Over the weekend, she decided to meet Trisha, after she had received her call.

Sara looked into the mirror, wondering if she should change her clothes for her meeting with Trisha. She had just returned from the office, and the navy blue long-sleeved shirt accompanied by black trousers looked perfectly well. She took her bag, called Trisha on her cell phone, as she walked out through the apartment door.

Sara reached the coffee shop and found Trisha sitting in a corner. "Hey," Sara said as she hugged Trisha.

"Something really unbelievable happened today," Trisha said.

"What?" Sara asked.

"I don't know how I should start," Trisha said, "a guy came to my house today, and he told me that he was a private detective, sent by someone related to you."

"What?" Sara said in confusion.

"He paid all the money that I have," Trisha halted finding the right words, "helped you with."

Sara went completely blank, and Trisha continued, "I asked him who he was working for, and he said that his employer didn't want his identity to be revealed."

"How much money did he give you?" Sara asked, without expression.

"Everything," Trisha said. "I told him that I can't take the money, but he said he wouldn't know what to do with the money then, as he was only a middle-man and his job was to make sure that I got the money." Trisha paused, expecting a reaction from Sara.

Sara remained in a state of shock for a while, and Trisha ordered hot coffee for both.

"And then what happened?" Sara asked in confusion.

"I told him no. But then he told me that whoever the provider is, he really loves you and is doing it only because he cares about you. Now I know how that feels, Sara; I love you too, and when I heard that someone is trying to help you, I understood." Trisha said.

"And who do you think the provider is?" Sara asked.

"Your parents, maybe. Who else is there?" Trisha said. "He also told me that if we tried to contact the provider he or she would completely deny it."

"I haven't spoken to them in so long." Sara spoke softly, almost whispering. "Could it be Ashish?"

"Why would it be Ashish? He openly denied you any help. He is the reason why your life has become hell." Trisha said, her voice rising in anger.

"Why didn't you call me?" Sara asked, ignoring Trisha's words.

"He said he would leave if I called you. That this meeting had nothing to do with you, even though it was about you. He was very convincing," she said, taking a pause.

"I have to go," Sara said, standing up.

"Where are you going?"

"Home. I need to go home. I am so sorry, but please understand."

"I do," Trisha said, giving her a light hug.

Sara decided to walk to her apartment, and throughout the walk, wondered if she should call her parents. Many thoughts arose and by the time she reached her apartment, she was sobbing. She entered her room and sat on the couch, looking at the phone and thinking: "If they wanted to help, why didn't they do it directly? If they know about my financial condition, they also know about my marriage." And she wondered, if they knew everything and still hadn't called, it implied that they did not want to talk to her. But contrary to all these thoughts, she was dying to hear their voices, after all, they were the only people left in the world with the title of family.

She picked up the phone and dialled her father's cell phone number.

"Hello!" Her father answered.

"Hello, dad!" Sara said, stopping herself from crying.

"Trisha?"

"Yep, how many other people call you 'dad'?" She said in a breaking voice.

"I am sorry. Where are you?" He asked in a serious voice.

"I am in Mumbai."

"Are you okay?"

"Yep, dad. I am fine. How is mum doing and how are you?" she asked.

"We are okay." He paused "How is everything? And how is Ashish?"

She took a deep breath, "Everything is okay, dad," she said and hung up. She went and lay down on her bed. She picked up a large pillow, hugged it tightly and cried without a sound and slept.

The next morning, Sara had a brief conversation with Trisha on the phone, after which they met in the afternoon. She stayed with her the entire day, discussing her job, divorce, and her phone conversation the previous night with her dad.

The next day, she went to work, and was sent to an Institute to lecture on Decision Making, Career Choices, and similar topics. She was accompanied by three male colleagues. She came back home in the evening and hadn't had anything to eat except for cups of tea and snacks. She ordered south -Indian food for herself and read *The Motorcycle Diaries* after which she slept.

She woke up at seven in the morning and followed her routine. Returning home from her office, she stopped by at Trisha's place to have dinner with her and her husband. During the dinner, Trisha told her that she was moving to the US in two months. Sara came back to her place and read her book, after which she slept.

As the days passed by and she worked harder and harder, she started to think about going back to college and resume her studies. She spent a lot of time, between sleeping and reading the book, thinking about her life: not in the retrospective mode, but about the future. After a month, on a bright Sunday, after she had had her breakfast, the door bell of her apartment rang. She opened the door and found a tall young man in formal attire holding a light briefcase, standing in front of her. "How may I help you?" Sara asked.

He told her his name and said: "Mrs Sara, I am a lawyer and I need to talk to you about something very important."

"About what?" Sara asked, nonplussed.

"It's very complicated in my position to explain everything standing here," he said. "May I come in?"

Sara didn't know what to answer. She let the lawyer enter her apartment. He observed the living room and walked straight to the table, upon which he kept his briefcase and opened it. She stood at the door all this while, watching him as he took out a packet, keys, and an envelope from his briefcase. "Mrs Sara," he said, "first of all, before I begin to explain the reason why I am here, I want you to understand I am only a representative. So, there are limitations to the information I can provide you with, are we clear on that?" He asked, politely.

"Go on," Sara said, trying to understand.

"A week ago, my client, Mr Ayan passed away" he said. "Before he died he prepared a will, according to which, you, now possess the ownership of his house in New

Delhi, as well as the money he used to earn as royalties from his books." He looked at the things he had kept on the table and said, "These are all the things he wanted you to have."

Sara was totally confused at this moment. "I don't know any Mr Ayan."

"I am aware of that," he said. She walked to the sofa which was neatly aligned around the table and sat there. "I think you have the wrong person," she said, confused.

"No, Mrs Sara, you are the right person," he said.

"Why would a person bequeath all his belongings to a stranger?"

The lawyer sighed, "I don't have the answer to that. But I know how you can find the answer to that."

"How?"

"He has left you a letter, which explains everything. But the letter is in Delhi, in the apartment."

"Why?" She asked.

"I don't know." He closed his briefcase preparing to leave. He took out his wallet, and took out a card from it. "This is my personal card," he said, keeping it on the table next to the papers. "I am leaving for Delhi in two days. You can have all these papers checked by your lawyers, whomever you want, and we can complete the formalities. Think about it, and if you need any more information, you can give me a call anytime." He smiled and left.

Sara called the lawyer in the evening and they both met at a coffee shop.

"For how long did you know him?" She asked.

"Only for a week before he died," Mezz replied. "What about you, have you read his books?"

"Yes I have I have read two of his novels," she replied. "I even met him two years ago."

"Where?"

"We met at a book-store. It was a book signing, and I went there especially for the event. I can remember him so clearly."

Mezz remained quiet as it was hard for him to talk about Ayan and remain expressionless at the same time.

"Can I ask you something?" Sara asked. "You probably might know something about this, considering you were his lawyer."

"Sure." Mezz said.

"Did he ever help me financially?"

Mezz remained quiet, thinking of what to say. "What difference would it make now? He is deceased. But if it makes you feel any better, then yes, he did. What have you decided? When will you come to Delhi?"

"In a couple of days." Sara said. "The thing is, I have to find out. I want to know who he was. What's the connection? Why would he give his home and all the money to me?"

They met again after a week in Delhi, with the purpose of visiting the house in which Ayan used to live.

"I have had the rooms cleaned up," Mezz said, as he opened the door "You have an extra set of keys?" Sara asked, standing behind him.

"No, I had it cleaned before I handed them to you. Ayan asked me to." Mezz lied. Of course he had the keys.

He opened the door and she entered the apartment behind him. Mezz switched on the lights of the empty hall. "What happened to the furniture?" Sara asked, impulsively.

Mezz smiled and said, "Oh, there was no furniture here. He lived alone, so everything he needed is in his room. Come, I'll show you," he said, walking straight to his room. "That other room is locked, I hope you understand why!"

Sara nodded as she followed him into the room and found a couch placed, facing the window, with piles of books scattered everywhere. There was a computer kept against the wall in front of her, aligned closer to the bed, creating a gap in the left corner between the bed and the computer. She sighed and sat on the bed while Mezz picked up the scattered books, which were not too many, and kept them on the computer desk.

"So," he said, "any thoughts?"

"It's beautifully designed." she said.

"His uncle has already taken his belongings," Mezz said. "It's only books, the computer, the bed, the couch, the fridge, all the stuff in the kitchen, and the souvenir he wanted you to have, that is left in this apartment."

Sara nodded. Mezz walked to the corner between the computer and the bed and opened a box which Sara hadn't noticed until now. He took out a bag and kept it on the floor next to her feet. "This is it," he said.

She reached inside the bag and took out a diary and countless sheets of papers properly arranged in a sequence. "*A thousand letters*" She read the text on the cover of the black diary, and turned to look at the sheets of paper. "February 21, 2004. Dearest, truly speaking, I can't think of a word right now. I have been thinking about what to say, writing it, and then re-writing it." She read the first line of the handwritten letter and looked at Mezz. "2004?" She asked in confusion.

"I think I should leave now," Mezz said. "I have ordered some food for you, I hope you like Chinese. The guy will be here shortly. If I may ask, where are you staying?"

"At a hotel." She replied, flipping through the pages of the diary.

"Why don't you stay here?"

"I don't know," she said, hesitatingly.

"Sara," Mezz said, "this is your house. You stay here, okay?"

She nodded in confusion. "You have my number. Call me if you need any help. Have a nice day," he said and left. She kept the diary down and continued reading the letter. After she finished the first letter, she realized that each letter was arranged according to its date. She lay down on the bed and kept reading the letters until the doorbell rang. She opened the door and received her food, and also took the phone number of the restaurant from the delivery boy. She took out two water bottles from the fridge kept in the kitchen and walked back to the room, but this time, she sat on the couch looking at the sky. She ate her food, after which she walked about the house, looking at things and found a pack of cigarettes and a cigarette lighter in the kitchen. She lit up a cigarette, sat on the couch and started reading the letters again.

After three hours of continuous reading, she kept the letters down and sat there thinking. She was not confused any more. Later that night, she slept after reading almost two hundred letters. In the morning, she went to her hotel and took whatever luggage she had brought with her, and checked out. She called Mezz on her way back and they both met at a coffee shop not far from the apartment.

"How are you?" he asked. "And how was last night?"

"It was good." She said. "Everything is clear now."

They both remained silent for a while, focusing on their coffee. Sara clearly wanted to talk about the letters, except she had no one who knew about this situation as much as Mezz did.

"So, what are you plans now?" he asked.

"My plan is to go back to studies. Also travel for a while. But not with his money."

"Why not?"

"It's complicated," she said, and Mezz nodded. "He helped me when I needed it the most. There's a wisdom behind that, to help someone without a selfish motive."

"Wow," Mezz uttered, "you talk like him too." He

smiled and she smiled back. "I think it's time I moved back to Delhi now. I have to start a new life, a life for myself."

"What about your job in Mumbai?" he asked.

"I'll find a job here in Delhi."

Mezz listened to her, smiling as he observed the strong individuality in her voice. He liked her and respected the fact that his friend's legacy had fallen into the right hands.

"Pardon me for asking," he said, "but what do you plan to do with his money if not use it for your own self? After all, that is what he intended."

"That may have been his intention but he was so unselfish. If his intentions weren't selfish, then how could mine be? He was a writer. I am sure if I give this money for someone's education who can't afford it, Ayan's intentions will be kept alive."

Mezz could not breathe and felt a heaviness in his chest that showed on his face, as he felt that the words she uttered came directly from Ayan's heart. He could not believe what he was hearing but at this exact moment he suddenly knew true love existed.

After they finished the coffee, Sara came back to the apartment with her luggage. She called one of her colleagues and told her that she wouldn't be coming to the office for four or five days, as she planned to stay in Delhi for a few days more. She took a long shower, after which she lit up a smoke, sat on the couch, and picked up Ayan's diary. She ordered some food for herself and continued reading the entire day, and the entire night, and slept in the morning.

She had read almost all the letters in three days, except only the last ones. She had deprived herself of sleep in the last two days, but even though extremely tired, she was filled with such strong emotions from reading those letters that she couldn't possibly think of sleeping. She looked outside the window and noticed the lemon tree, which caught her attention for a moment. She went to the kitchen and made coffee for herself, after which she picked up the remaining letters and started reading them. She finally opened the last letter and started reading it:

> Dearest,
>
> Considering the current situation, perhaps of unforeseen reality and a dubious clarity, I presume that you are surprised as well as calm. Patience is one of the greatest virtues, so, I leave the conclusion to you. I am ashes now, which is the sole reason why you're reading this.
>
> I would like to talk to you a bit differently today; perhaps in full honesty, I would confess that I have been studying your life very closely. These last days of my life have been completely compromised in your thoughts. And I must also confess that I was rather worried about you.
>
> I have often wondered: What is achievement? A wise person would say: It's satisfaction. But is

it the truth? Honestly, I have no clue. A man's achievements cannot dictate his heart. His history can never tell those personal thoughts. His texts can neither reveal the joy when he wrote them, nor the tears. An able man's thoughts are of two types: those which give him pride; and those which he fears the most. The former transforms into his ideologies, and the latter into disbelief, skepticism or sorrow. Emotions, on the other hand, are the dearest possession of a man, and the first to get buried and forgotten with the man's body.

My love, the subjection of pain in a man's life is supremely based upon the number of wants he places ahead. It's a very simple rule; for example: a man, who strives to achieve something, simultaneously faces the possibility to meet failure. One, who invites love, unknowingly invites rejection too.

Which is why the only true state a man should strive to achieve is the state of consciousness. And consciousness can only be achieved by detachment—not from the world, but from the minds of those who hold you back.

And now to my greatest discovery–What is love?

Love is not a necessity; it's a choice. It's not a dying necessity, in which one simply throws away every possibility of a personal evolution of his mind. Then it only becomes selfish love, in which you want the person at any cost. And not only selfish, but self-destructive. I hope you will understand my words, my angel. One should strive to achieve the greatest of goals, and love must be present in all of them, but not as a hindering agent, but a motivating one. So again, don't make love a necessity, that you can't live without it; treat every element of your life with the respect in its own frame. Love should be followed, but not when it leads to destruction. A man's focus, in the entire term of his life, should strongly connect with the principle that he must never lose touch with rationality.

And at last, about us. If you wish to seek true happiness, you shall do charity. If you wish to be wealthy, then labour. If you wish prosperity, then master the art of patience. If you wish to seek the truth, then listen to your mind and never your heart. And if you wish to find love, then, my angel, remember me.

Goodbye.

Ayan